Nancy

Maeve Binchy was born in Dublin, and went to school at the Holy Child Convent in Killiney. She took a history degree at UCD and taught in various girls' schools, writing travel articles in the long summer holidays. In 1969 she joined the *Irish Times*. For the last ten years she has been based in London and writes humorous columns from all over the world. The Peacock Theatre in Dublin was the scene of her two stage plays, *End of Term* and *Half Promised Land,* and her television play, *Deeply Regretted By,* won two Jacobs Awards and the Best Script Award at the Prague Film Festival. She is the author of three other volumes of short stories, *Central Line, Victoria Line* and *Dublin 4,* as well as two novels, *Light a Penny Candle* and *Echoes*. Maeve Binchy is married to the writer and broadcaster Gordon Snell.

Also in Arrow by Maeve Binchy

Dublin 4

THE
LILAC BUS

Maeve Binchy

ARROW BOOKS

Arrow Books Limited
62-65 Chandos Place, London WC2N 4NW

An imprint of Century Hutchinson Limited

London Melbourne Sydney Auckland
Johannesburg and agencies throughout
the world

First published by Ward River Press Ltd,
Co. Dublin, 1984
Century hardcover edition 1986
Arrow edition 1987

Printed and bound in Great Britain by
Anchor Brendon Limited, Tiptree, Essex

ISBN 0 09 950290 9

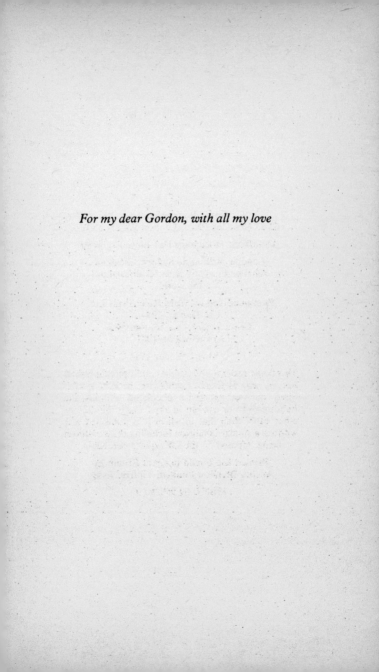

For my dear Gordon, with all my love

Contents

Nancy was early, but then she always was, and she didn't like being seen there too soon. It looked as if you had nothing else to do if you arrived far too early for the bus home. The others all arrived rushing and panting and afraid they'd miss it, because if they missed it then they really did. Tom turned the key in the ignition at 6.45 and swung the Lilac Bus out into the road. That way he had them all home before ten o'clock and that was his promise. No point in going home for a weekend if you aren't in the pub by ten, that was his philosophy. It wasn't Nancy's but she was compulsively early for everything. It was just her way. She went into a shop that sold magazines and cards. She knew a lot of the cards by heart from studying them on a Friday. There was the big one with tears falling down it: "Sorry I missed your birthday." They had the country papers in this shop too but Nancy never bought one. There'd be a paper at home and she could catch up on everything then.

She examined her new perm in the big round mirror which was not meant so much as a mirror as a deterrent to shoplifting. It was set high on the wall and at a funny angle, or she hoped it was. Otherwise the perm looked very odd indeed. She stared up at her reflection anxiously. Surely she didn't look like some small worried animal with fuzzy hair and huge terrified eyes. That's what she saw in the mirror, but of course that's not what people down at her own level would see? After all, everyone looked silly from this point of view. She patted her head and had another pang about the perm. It looked to her dangerously like those old-fashioned perms that people like her mother got in Rathdoon. The summer perm and the Christmas perm. Frizz, fuzz . . . tight curls growing out into what looked like flashes of lightning or electric shocks as the weeks went by. The girls in the salon assured her that she was mad to think this. She had got a modern perm, one of the newest on the market. Think what she'd have paid if she had to pay for it! Nancy had smiled grimly. Paid for it! At that price! Nancy Morris wouldn't have paid half that price or a quarter of that price for a perm. Nancy Morris had crossed Dublin to go to a salon where she heard they needed people to practise on. *Models* was the expression, but Nancy was more realistic. They needed heads with hair and smart people like Nancy found out which were the big salons with lots of trainees and on what nights their classes and demonstrations were. She had only paid for two visits to a hairdresser since she came to Dublin six years ago. That wasn't bad going, she smiled proudly. Still it was done now, this perm, no point in peering up at herself and worrying. Better go across and get on the bus. Surely some of the others would be there by now, and it was well after half-past six.

Tom was sitting there reading an evening paper. He looked up and smiled. "Evening, Miss Mouse," he said pleasantly and lifted her big suitcase up onto the roof rack with one easy movement. She got in crossly. She *hated* him calling her Miss Mouse, but it was her own fault. When she had rung to ask for a place in his minibus she had given her name as Miss Morris. Well, she was used to being formal on the phone – that was what her job was about, for heaven's sake. How was she to know that she should have said her first name and that he genuinely misheard the Morris bit. But it was very galling that he still refused to call her Nancy, even though he always called old Mrs Hickey Judy and she could have been his mother.

12

"It's light for such a big case," he said pleasantly. Nancy just nodded. She didn't feel like telling him it was her only suitcase and she had no intention of going out and spending over a fiver on some kind of nylon holdall like the others had. And anyway she needed a big case: there were always things to take back to Dublin, like potatoes and whatever vegetables there were, and anything else that turned up. There was the time that her mother's friend, Mrs Casey, was getting rid of her curtains: Nancy brought them back and they were lovely in the flat.

She sat down in one of the middle seats, straightened her skirt under her so that it wouldn't crease and took out her glucose sweets. They had jars of them in the hospital, and they always told her to help herself. She didn't eat them normally but it was nice on a bus journey to have something; the others often bought barley sugar or toffees, but what was the point of spending money on sweets when they were there for the asking? She unfolded a newspaper that one of the patients had left behind in the waiting room. She got a lot of her reading material this way – people waiting for the specialists were inclined to be forgetful about papers and magazines, and there was rarely an evening she didn't have something to read. And it was nice to have a variety, she told herself. It was like a surprise. Mairead didn't understand. Nancy's brow darkened when she thought of Mairead. And all that had to be sorted out. It had been so unexpected and so unfair.

She held up the newspaper so that Tom would think she was reading and she went over it all again. Mairead coming in on Wednesday and walking round restlessly picking things up and putting them down. You didn't have to be a genius to know there was something on her mind. Nancy thought she was going to ask about the television again. They had a perfectly good black and white set which was a bit snowstormish now and then but usually got a terrific reception. What on earth was the point of paying out a fortune renting a colour set? And even a video: Mairead had once mentioned this as if they were some kind of millionaires. She had looked up from the telly, which was admittedly having one of its bad nights and you had to guess a lot from the soundtrack; but Mairead had wanted to talk about something much bigger.

"I've been thinking all week at work how to say this, Nancy, and I can't think of any proper way so I'll just say it straight out. I want to share the flat with someone else, and I am going to have to ask you to leave. In your own time of course, I'm not throwing you out on the road ... " She had given a little nervous laugh but Nancy had been too astounded to join in. "You see," Mairead had gone on, "it was never permanent. It was just to see what we thought .... that was the arrangement. That was what we said ... " Her voice had trailed away guiltily.

"But we've been sharing for three years," Nancy said.

"I know," Mairead said miserably.

"So·why? Don't I pay the rent in time always and the electricity? And I contribute to the food from home and I got curtains for the hall windows and ... ?

"Of course, Nancy, nobody's saying you didn't."

"So why?"

"It's just ... no there's no reason, can't we do it nice and easily now without quarrels and questions. Can't you just find another place and we'll still meet now and then, go to the pictures, you come over here one evening, me go to your place. Come on, Nancy, that's the grown-up way to do things."

Nancy had burned with rage. Mairead, who worked in a flower shop, telling her what was the grown-up way to do things. Mairead who hadn't got one honour in her Leaving Certificate ordering Nancy out of her flat. *Her* flat. True, she had found it, and when she needed someone to share the rent her aunt Mrs Casey, the friend of Nancy's mother, had suggested Nancy. Where had Mairead got these notions and more important, why? Who did she want to share with?

The worst thing was that Mairead didn't seem to know

14

or care, she just said she would like a change. At this point Nancy had turned off the flickering telly and had settled in for what she thought was going to be a heart-to-heart where Mairead would tell her all about some star-crossed love. But no. Mairead was busy looking at the calendar. Would we say just over a month, like the middle of October? That would surely give her time to find somewhere.

"But who will I share with?" Nancy had wailed.

Mairead had shrugged. She didn't know, maybe Nancy could get a bed-sit on her own. She didn't do much cooking or entertaining, a bed-sit might be just as good. But they cost a *fortune!* Mairead had shrugged again as if it didn't concern her.

The following morning Nancy was having her tea in the kitchen – she never bothered with a breakfast since there was always food in the hospital, and what was the point of being a receptionist for all these doctors unless you got some perks like a canteen and glucose sweets? Mairead rushed in late as usual and Nancy asked her had she forgiven her.

"Forgive you, Nancy? What for? What in heaven's name for?"

"Well I must have done something, otherwise you wouldn't be asking me to leave our flat."

"It's *my* flat and don't be such a clown. We're not married to each other, Nancy. You came in here to share my rent, now that bit's over. Right? Yes. That's all there is to it." She was gulping down a bowl of cornflakes and trying to pull on her boots at the same time. Mairead loved these boots; they horrified Nancy – they had cost a week's salary. For a pair of boots.

"What'll I tell them in Rathdoon?" Nancy asked solemnly. Mairead was startled.

"About what?" she had asked, bewildered.

"About us breaking up?"

"Sure who would want to know? Who even knows we share a flat?"

"Everyone: your mother, my mother, your aunt Mrs

Casey, everyone."

"Well, what do you mean what will you tell them?" Mairead was genuinely surprised.

"But your mother, what will she think? What will I tell her?"

Mairead had lost her temper suddenly. Nancy still felt a shock just thinking about it.

"My mother is a normal woman; she's like everyone else's mother, including your mother. She doesn't think anything. She wants to know that I'm not pregnant and I'm not on drugs and I'm still going to Mass. That's all any mother wants to know in the name of God, those same three things. In India mothers want to know that or Russia or wherever, and it may not be mass for them but it's something. People's mothers don't give two flying damns about their daughters sharing flats with people and whether they get on well or whether as in our case they drive each other up the wall. They just want to be told the essentials."

"We don't drive each other up the wall," Nancy had said quietly.

"No, well, irritate each other. What's the difference. Why bother your head explaining and telling and reporting back. People aren't bloody interested."

"Do I irritate you?"

"Yes."

"How?"

"Oh Nancy, *please.*" Mairead was stricken. "We agreed last night to be grown-up and not to have pointless rows and recriminations. We agreed. Now look what you're starting. Of course people irritate each other. I probably drive you mad. Listen, I must go."

Nancy had a terrible day: she had looked at the prices of flats and bed-sitters and they were sky high. The further out you went they came down a bit of course, but she had to be within cycling distance of the hospital. There was no way she was going to spend her hard-earned money on bus fares. She had thought too about what Mairead had said. She couldn't think why she was irritating. She didn't smoke, she never invited rowdy people in like Mairead often did, people who brought a bottle of wine each and then went out for chicken and chips. She didn't play records loud – she didn't have any records. She did everything to help. Often she cut special offers out of the paper and collected vouchers for foods or detergents. She suggested often to Mairead that it would be cheaper to come home every weekend to Rathdoon because people spend a fortune at weekends in Dublin and you could live free at home. How had she been so irritating?

Even this very morning she had asked Mairead if it was definite, and Mairead had nodded wordlessly. Nancy had offered to let Mairead have the weekend to consider her decision but in a low soft voice, unlike her harangue of the previous morning, Mairead had said there would be no considering and she realised that Nancy would be co-operative and start looking for another place straight away.

She looked up at the sound of voices. Dee Burke had arrived; she wore her college scarf even though she had left UCD two years previously, and she carried a canvas grip which she threw up on the roof herself. Tom was laughing at her.

"You'll be a discus champion yet," he said.

"No, it's to show you that women are genuinely liberated, that's all – besides there's nothing in it except a couple of pairs of knickers and some law books I'm meant to be studying."

Nancy was amazed that Dee, who was Dr Burke's daughter and lived in a big house covered with creeper could talk about knickers to Tom Fitzgerald in such a relaxed way. It didn't even sound rude the way she said it. Dee was a law unto herself though and always had been. You'd think she'd have her own car but she said that she wasn't earning much as a Solicitor's apprentice. Still Nancy would have thought that this minibus would have been beneath the Burkes. They were people of such standing in

Rathdoon, they must find it strange that their daughter travelled with anyone and everyone. Dee never seemed to notice. She was friendly with everyone, with that tinker of a fellow Kev Kennedy that you'd try to cross the road to avoid, with desperate Mikey Burns and his dirty jokes. Dee was specially nice to Nancy; she came and sat beside her and asked, as she often did, about Nancy's work.

It was quite extraordinary the way Dee remembered the names of the doctors she worked for, and knew that one was an eye specialist, one an orthopaedic surgeon and one an ear, nose and throat man. She knew there was Mr Barry and Mr White and Mr Charles. Even Nancy's mother wouldn't know that, and as for Mairead she could hardly remember the names of her own bosses let alone Nancy's.

But then Dee was nice and she had great breeding. People like that were courteous, Nancy always thought and they had the manners to be interested in other people.

Rupert Green arrived next. He was wearing a very smart jacket.

"Merciful God, Rupert, is that Italian? Is that the real thing?" Dee asked, feeling the sleeve as Rupert got in.

"Yes it is actually." Rupert's pale face flushed with pleasure. "How did you know?"

"Aren't I worn out looking at them in magazines. It's gorgeous."

"Yes, it's a second, or a discontinued line or something, but a friend got it for me anyway." Rupert was very pleased that it had caused such a stir.

"Well, they'd need to be a second or something, otherwise your father would have to sell his practice to buy it," Dee laughed. Rupert's father was the solicitor, and it was through Mr Green she had got her apprenticeship in Dublin. Nancy looked at them enviously. It must be great to have such an easy way of going on. It was like a kind of shorthand in professional families, she noticed, they could all talk to each other at the drop of a hat. She felt a twinge of annoyance that her father, long dead, had been a postman and not a lawyer. The annoyance was followed by a stronger twinge of guilt. Her father had worked long and hard and had been pleased to see them all do well at their books and get secretarial or clerical jobs.

Rupert went to the back seat and almost on cue Mrs Hickey arrived. Suntanned even in winter she looked healthy and strong and as if she might be any age. Nancy knew she must be in her late fifties, but that was only by questioning people and piecing it all together. Judy Hickey worked in some kind of mad place that sold herbal cures and grain and nuts, and she even grew some of the things herself which was why she came home every week end to harvest them and bring them back to this shop in Dublin. Nancy had never been to the shop; Dee told her it was marvellous, that everyone should go and see it just for the experience of it but Nancy took her position as receptionist to three of Dublin's leading consultants very seriously. It wouldn't do for her to be seen going in and out of some quack's shop, would it?

Judy went to sit beside Rupert in the back and Mikey Burns had begun to squeeze himself in to the front seat. Laughing and rubbing his hands he told them a joke about hairy tennis balls. Everyone smiled and Mikey seemed to be able to settle down now that he had told at least one dirty story. He looked out eagerly.

"Will I be lucky and get the beautiful Celia beside me or do I get Mr Kennedy? Oh dear, just your luck Mikey, here comes Mr Kennedy."

Kev sneaked into the bus looking over his shoulder as if he expected a guard to lay a hand on him and say *Just a minute* like they do in films. Nancy thought she had never seen anyone who looked so furtive. If you spoke to Kev Kennedy he jumped a foot in the air, and he never said much in reply so he wasn't spoken to much.

And lastly Celia came. Big and sort of handsome in a way, though Nancy didn't admire those kind of looks. She often wore tight belts; as she wore them when she was nursing, she had probably got used to them. They made her figure very obvious. Not sexy, but it certainly divided it for all to see: a jutting out top half in front and a big jutting out bottom half at the back. Nancy would have thought she might have been wiser to wear something more floppy.

Celia sat in beside Tom: the last person always sat beside the driver. It was only twenty to seven and they set off with five minutes in hand.

"I have you very well trained," Tom laughed as he nosed the minibus out into the Friday evening traffic.

"Indeed you have. No wee-wees until we're across the Shannon," said Mikey looking round for approval, and since he didn't hear any he said it again. This time a few people smiled back at him.

Nancy told Dee all about Mr Charles and Mr White and Mr Barry and how they saw their private patients on certain days of the week and how she kept their appointment books and shuffled people around and how patients were often very grateful to her and gave her little presents at Christmas. Dee wanted to know were they well thought of, the doctors, and whether people praised them. Nancy tried to dredge examples but couldn't. She was more on the administrative side, she kept insisting. Dee wanted to know whether she met them socially, and Nancy had laughed to think such a thing was possible. That was the joy of being a doctor's daughter, you didn't think class distinctions existed any more. No, of course she didn't get involved in their home lives. Mr Barry had a Canadian wife and two children, Mr White's wife was a teacher and they had four children, and Mr Charles and his wife had no children. Yes, she sometimes spoke to their wives on the phone; they all seemed very nice, they all remembered her name. "Hallo Miss Morris," they would say.

Dee fell asleep when Nancy was explaining about the hospital switchboard which was very awkward and how they had been looking for a separate switchboard for the consultants for ages, but maybe things would get better with the new set-up in the phone headquarters. Nancy was a bit embarrassed at that. Maybe she had been rabbitting on, possibly she did irritate people by talking too much about little things; sometimes her own mother got up and went to bed in the middle of one of their conversations. Mairead might be right. But no, that couldn't be, Dee had been positively pressing her for details of her working life, she had asked question after question. No, Nancy couldn't blame herself for being boring. Not this time. She sighed and looked at the fields flying by.

Soon she nodded off too. Behind her Judy Hickey and Rupert Green were talking about someone they knew who had gone to an Ashram in India and everyone had to wear yellow or saffron. In front of her Kev Kennedy was half-listening as Mikey Burns explained a card trick with a glass of water. Mikey said that it was better if you saw it done but you could still grasp the point if you concentrated.

In front of them Tom was saying something to Celia; she was nodding and agreeing with it, whatever it was. It was very comfortable and warm, and even if she did lean over a bit in sleep and slump on top of Dee, well it didn't matter. She wouldn't have let herself doze if she were beside one of the men. Or indeed beside Judy Hickey: there was something very odd about her.

Nancy was asleep.

Her mother was still at the kitchen table when she got in. She was writing a letter to her daughter in America.

"There you are," she said.

"All in one piece," said Nancy.

It wasn't much of a greeting between mother and daughter when the whole country had been crossed. But they had never been a demonstrative family. No hugging and kissing, no linking arms.

"How was the journey?" her mother asked.

"Oh, the same. I had a bit of a sleep so I have a crick in

my neck." Nancy rubbed it thoughtfully.

"It's great to be able to sleep on that road, with maniacs screeching past you in all directions."

"Oh, it's not that bad." Nancy looked around. "Well, what's been happening?"

Her mother was poor at handing out news. Nancy would have liked her to get up, wet a pot of tea and come back full of detail and information. She wanted to hear the week's events and who had been home, who had been heard from, who had revealed what. But somehow it was never like that.

"Whatever happens? Nothing's been happening – weren't you here until Sunday night?" Her mother went back to the letter, sighing, "Do you never write to Deirdre at all? Wouldn't it be a Christian thing to write to your own sister in America and tell her what's going on? She loves to hear little things you know."

"So do I, but you can never remember anything to tell me!" Nancy cried in complaint.

"Ah, will you stop that nonsense, sure aren't you here the whole time? You only go up to Dublin for a couple of days in the week. Poor Deirdre's on the other side of the Atlantic Ocean."

"Poor Deirdre has a husband and three children and a freezer and an icebox and a sprinkler in her garden. Poor Deirdre indeed."

"Couldn't you have all that yourself if you wanted to? Stop grudging things to your sister. Have some bit of niceness in you."

"I've plenty of niceness." Nancy felt her lip tremble.

"Well stop giving out about Deirdre then, and go on, take a sheet of paper and put it in with mine. It'll save you getting a stamp and everything."

Her mother shoved a writing pad across the table. Nancy hadn't even sat down yet. The big suitcase with the hard corners was in the middle of the floor. She felt this was a shabby welcome home, but she was also a practical person. If she scribbled off a page to Deirdre now, well it

22

would save her having to do it some other time, and it would please her mother who might go and bring out some soda bread and apple tart if she was in a good humour. Nancy wrote a few lines hoping that Deirdre and Sean and Shane and April and Erin were all well, and saying she'd love to come over and see them all but the fares were desperate and it was much easier for them to come over this way because of the pound and the dollar. She told Deirdre about Mr White's new car, and Mr Charles going to Russia on his holidays and Mr Barry's wife having a new handbag that was made from the skin of a baby crocodile and had cost what you wouldn't believe. She added that it was nice to get back to Rathdoon at weekends because... She paused at this point. It was nice to get back to Rathdoon because... She looked at her mother sitting at the table frowning over the letter writing. No, that wasn't why she came home. Her mother was only mildly pleased, and if she wasn't here there was the television or Mrs Casey or the bingo or half a dozen other things. Sometimes on the long summer evenings, Nancy had come home and found the house empty and her mother out at ten o'clock. She didn't come home for the dance like Celia did, or Kev or Mikey on the bus. She had not got what you'd call friends in Rathdoon.

She finished the letter, "It's nice to get back at the weekends because the Lilac Bus is really very good value and you'd spend a small fortune in Dublin over the weekend without even noticing it."

Her mother was packing up for bed. No tea, no apple tart.

"I think I'll just make myself a sandwich," Nancy said.

"Did you have no tea? Aren't you very disorganised for a high-up receptionist?" said her mother, who went to bed without a word of goodnight.

It was a bright sunny September Saturday. The tourists were mainly gone but there were always a few golfers around. Nancy wandered up the street with no plan. She could have bought a newspaper and gone to the hotel to have coffee, but apart from the money altogether she wouldn't do that. It was being uppity going in there sitting as if you were the type. No. She saw Celia's mother washing the step of the pub. She looked older, her face was lined like that gypsy-looking Judy Hickey's. She called out a greeting, but Celia's mother didn't hear, she kept scrubbing. Nancy wondered was Celia still in bed or was she helping to clean up inside. Celia worked weekends in the pub, that's why she came home. Her mother must have made it worth her while, because it was a hard job to stand on your feet all weekend there after having stood on your feet as a nurse all week. But you'd never know the time of day with Celia, she was so tight with information or anything at all. It was odd to see her talking away to Tom on the bus last night; usually she looked out the window with a moon face. Not like Dee, who was so full of life and so interested in everything. Nancy often wished that things were different, and that she could call on Dee at the weekend, or go off somewhere with her. But she wouldn't dream of going up to Burkes. Not in a million years would she call on the house. The surgery was a different matter, that was the way things were.

She passed Judy Hickey's cottage and saw signs of great activity out in the back. Big packing boxes were laid all round, and Judy was wearing old trousers and had her hair tied up in a scarf. The house itself was shabby and needed a coat of paint but the garden was immaculate. It was odd that so many people watered and weeded and kept the birds off for Mrs Hickey, Nancy thought; she wasn't the kind of woman that you'd think people would like at all. She only went to Mass one Sunday in four, if that. She never spoke of her husband and children. They had gone away years ago when the young lad was only a baby; Nancy could hardly remember the time there was children in that house. Anyway, up and away with the father and the two children and not a word out of the mother. She never got the court to give them back to her; people had said there must be some fine secrets there that they didn't want to come out, otherwise she would surely have gone to law. And for years her working in this shop which sold things gurus used out in the East and things that must be disapproved of, ginseng and all that. Still Judy Hickey seemed to have more friends than a few. Even now there were two of Kev Kennedy's brothers helping her, and last week Mikey Burns was there with his shovel. Young Rupert would probably have been in the team but his father was very sick and that's why he had been coming home every weekend.

Nancy sighed and passed on. A half-thought that she might help too had come in one side of her mind but flashed quickly out the other. Why should she dig and get dirty in Judy Hickey's garden for nothing? She had better things to do. When she got back home and there was a note on the kitchen table, she wondered what better things she meant. Her mother had scribbled that Mrs Casey had called to take her for a spin. Mrs Casey had learned to drive late in life and had a dangerous-looking old car which was the joy of her heart. It had brightened life for many people including Nancy's mother; indeed there was talk of a few of them coming the whole way to Dublin in it. The plan had been that Mrs Casey and Mrs Morris would stay at the flat. After all, Mrs Casey was Mairead's aunt. Now there would be no flat and no Mairead. Nancy's heart lurched at the memory of it all.

And nothing for the lunch and no mention of when the spin would be over, and nothing much in the press or in the little fridge, nothing you could eat. Nancy put on two potatoes to boil and went across to Kennedys' shop.

"Can I have two small rashers, please?"

"Two pounds is it?" Kev Kennedy's father didn't listen much to people: he was always listening to the radio in the shop.

"No, just two single ones."

"Huh," he said picking two out and weighing them.

"You see my mother hasn't done the shopping yet so I

don't know what she wants."

"You can't go far wrong on two slices of bacon," Mr Kennedy agreed, morosely wrapping them in greaseproof paper and putting them in a bag. "She'll never accuse you of getting the family into debt over that."

She heard a laugh and to her annoyance noticed that Tom Fitzgerald was in the shop. For some reason she didn't like him hearing her being made fun of like that.

"Oh, Miss Mouse is a great one to live dangerously," he said.

Nancy managed a smile and went out.

The afternoon seemed long. There was nothing on the radio, and nothing to read. She washed her two blouses and put them out on the line. She remembered with great annoyance that nobody, not even her mother, had remarked on her perm. What was the point of getting one if people didn't notice? Paying good money for one of the newest perms. Well, paying money if she had had to: fortunately she hadn't. At six she heard the banging of car doors and voices.

"Oh, there you are, Nancy." Her mother always seemed surprised to see her. "Mrs Casey and I've been for a great drive altogether."

"Hallo Mrs Casey. That's nice," Nancy said grumpily.

"Did you get us any supper?" Her mother looked expectant.

"No. Well, you didn't say. There wasn't anything there." Nancy was confused.

"Oh, come on Maura, she's only joking. Surely you've something made for your mother, Nancy?"

Nancy hated Mrs Casey's arch voice treating her as if she was a slow-minded five-year-old.

"No, why should I have? There was no food there. I presumed my mam was getting something."

There was a silence.

"And there was nothing for lunch either," she said in an aggrieved tone. "I had to go over to Kennedy's to get

26

rashers."

"Well we'll have rashers for our supper," Mrs Morris brightened up.

"I've eaten them," Nancy said.

"All of them?" Mrs Casey was disbelieving.

"I only got two," she said.

There was another silence.

"Right," Mrs Casey said, "that settles it. I wanted your mother to come back with me but she said no, that you'd probably have the tea made for us all and she didn't want to disappoint you. I said it was far from likely, judging from what I'd heard. But she had to come back, nothing would do her." She was half way back to the door. "Come on, Maura, leave the young people be . . . . They have better things to do than getting tea for the likes of us." Nancy looked at her mother, whose face was set in a hard line of disappointment and shame.

"Enjoy your evening then, Nance," she said. And they were gone. The car was starting with a series of jumps and leaps.

What could Mrs Casey have heard, what did she mean? The only person she could have heard anything from was Mairead, or Mairead's mother. What could they have been saying – that Nancy was irritating? Was that it?

She didn't want to be in when they came back but where could she go? She had arranged no lift to the dance: she would as soon be hanged as to go out on the straight road and hitch all the way to the night entertainment which she wouldn't enjoy anyway. She supposed she could always go to Ryan's pub. She'd be bound to know people and it was her own home town and she was twenty-five years of age so she could do what she liked. She put on one of her freshly cleaned blouses which she ironed with great care. She decided the perm was an undoubted success and gave herself a spray of the perfume she had bought her mother last Christmas and set out.

It wasn't bad in Ryan's; some of the golfing people were buying big rounds, shouting at each other from the counter: what did you want with the vodka, Brian, did you want water with the Power's, Derek? Celia was behind the counter helping her mother.

"You don't usually come in here," Celia said.

"It's a free country and I'm over twenty-one," Nancy said snappishly.

"Oh Jesus, take it easy," Celia had said. "It's too early for the fights."

There was a phone in a booth and she saw Dee Burke making a call; their phone must be out of order at home. Nancy waved but Dee didn't see her. Biddy Brady who had been two classes below Nancy at school had got engaged and she was celebrating with a group of the girls. The ring was being passed around and admired. She waved Nancy over to the group, and rather than sit on her own she went.

"We're putting a sum into the kitty each and then the drinks keep coming and we pay for it until the money runs out," said one girl helpfully.

"Oh, I don't think I'll be here all that long," Nancy said hastily, and noticed a few odd looks being exchanged.

She waved at Mikey Burns who was carrying two drinks over to a corner.

"Have you any pub jokes?" Nancy asked, hoping he might stop and entertain them for a moment.

"Not tonight, Nancy," he said, and didn't even pause. Mikey! Who would do anything for an audience! He was heading for the corner, a woman with her head down sat there, it looked like Billy Burns' wife.

Billy was Mikey's brother, the one that got the looks and the brains and the luck people said.

There was a bit of commotion behind the bar and Celia's mother seemed to be shouting at her. It was hushed up but Celia looked very anxious. One of the Kennedy brothers had stepped in behind the bar to help wash glasses.

Nancy felt a bit dizzy. She had drunk two gins and

orange which she had bought for herself and two as part of Biddy Brady's celebration. She had had nothing to eat since lunchtime. She decided to get some fresh air and some chips in that order. She could always come back. She sat on the wall near the chip shop and ate them slowly. You could see the whole town from here: the Burkes' house with all that lovely creeper cut away from the windows so neatly. She thought she saw Dee leaning out a window smoking but it was darkish, she couldn't be certain. Then there was the Fitzgeralds' drapery, Tom's family's business. His two brothers and their wives worked there, as well as his father. They had a craft shop now attached to it, and they made up Irish tweeds into skirts for the visitors. Mrs Casey lived about a mile out so she couldn't glare at her windows and imagine her mother eating lamb chops and looking at television, counting the days with Mrs Casey until the *Late Late Show* came back from its summer break. When they had been planning the Dublin trip they had wanted Mairead and Nancy to get them tickets for the show, and Mairead had actually written and found out what the chances were. Nancy had thought it was madness of the first order.

It was chilly and the last chip was gone. She walked back to Ryan's and thought she would go in the side entrance and visit the Ladies' on the way. She nearly fell over Mrs Ryan who was sitting on the step.

"Oh, it's *Miss* Morris," the woman said with a very snide little laugh.

"Goodnight, Mrs Ryan," said Nancy a bit nervously.

"'Oh Miss Morris, Miss Mean Morris. Mean as all get out, they say about you."

She didn't sound drunk. Her voice was steady and cold.

"Who says that about me?" Nancy was equally cold.

"Everyone. Every single person who ever speaks your name. Poor Biddy Brady's crowd of girls, just to mention a few. You sat down and took a couple of spirits off them and walked off. That's class, Miss Morris, strong men have

29

wanted to be able to do that and they're not."

"Why do you call me Miss Morris?"

"Because that's what you call yourself, that's what you think you are. And by God that's the way you're going to stay. No man would take you on, Miss Morris, a mean woman is worse than a nag and a slut put together . . . ."

"I'll be off, I think, Mrs Ryan."

"Oh I would, Miss Morris; those little girls in there have had a few drinks now and if you haven't come back to put a couple of fivers into their kitty, I think you'd be far better to be off."

"Put *what* into their kitty?" Nancy was stunned.

"Oh, be off, Miss Morris, I beg of you."

But her blood was up now. She pushed past the woman and went into the smoke and heat.

"Sorry Biddy," she said loudly, "I went home for change. I hadn't my money with me. Can I put this into the kitty and I'm having a gin and orange when the round comes."

They looked at her in disbelief and with some guilt. Those who had been loudest against her were abashed.

"A large gin and orange for Nancy," they called and Celia who was working alone with only Bart Kennedy to help her raised her eyebrows. Nancy Morris ordering large ones.

"They cost a fair whack nowadays, Nancy," she said.

"Oh, for Christ's sake, will you give me a drink not a sermon," Nancy said and the others all laughed.

They were singing "By The River of Babylon, where I sat down," but Nancy was only mouthing the words.

Mean, Mean, Mean. That was what Mairead thought, what she told her mother and her aunt, why she wanted her out of the flat; that's what Mrs Casey thought, that's what her mother had felt tonight, that's what the Kennedys' father had been jeering at in the shop. That's what Celia meant now, talking about the price of a drink. That is what

Mrs Ryan, who must have gone stone mad tonight, meant, sitting on the floor of her own public house in the side entrance.

Mean.

But she wasn't mean: she was careful, she was sensible, she was not going to throw away her money. She was going to spend it on what she wanted. Which was... which was... Well, she didn't know yet. It certainly wasn't clothes, or a holiday or a car. And it wasn't on dear things to furnish rented accommodation, and it wasn't on going to dances or discos or to hotels with fancy prices. And it wasn't on smart hairdressers or Italian shoes or fillet steaks or a stereo radio with headphones.

They had linked arms now and they were singing "Sailing" and swaying from side to side. Mrs Ryan had come back and was singing with the best; in fact she was standing up in the middle of the circle and playing the Rod Stewart role with somebody's golf club as a microphone.

Celia was pulling pints still; she looked at her mother with neither embarrassment nor pride – it was just as if she were another customer. Tom Fitzgerald was talking to her over the bar. They were very thick, those two. Tears came down Nancy's face at Mrs Ryan's words. A mean woman. She wasn't at all mean. But if people *thought* she was, then she must be. Mustn't she?

Deirdre had once said she was a bit tight with money, but she had thought that was Deirdre, being all American and accusing people face to face of things. Her brother in Cork had once said that she must own massive property up in Dublin now, what with her earning a good salary and paying hardly a penny out a week except her rent and the Lilac Bus. She had said nonsense, that it cost a packet to live in Dublin. He had pointed out that she had a bicycle and she got a three-course meal in the hospital at midday, and what else did she spend it on? The conversation had ended fairly unsatisfactorily, she had thought. Now she realised that he was saying she was mean. Mean.

Suppose people *really* thought she was mean? Should she explain that it wasn't meanness, and she was only making sure she didn't throw money away? No, somehow it was one of those things that you couldn't explain. It was either there, the belief, or it wasn't there. And so, unfair as it was, she was now going to have to go overboard the other way.

Tomorrow she would suggest to her mother that she take them both to a nice Sunday lunch in the hotel as a treat. It was too late to do anything about Mairead, there was no promising to be more generous or to spend more or whatever it was people wanted. And maybe she could get some posters of Ireland and send them to Deirdre's children. Happy birthday Shane or April or Erin from your Auntie Nancy in the Emerald Isle. And to the silent brother in Cork, some book about fishing and a pressing invitation to visit her when next he came up for the Spring Show.

It must work: look at Biddy Brady's party, they were delighted with her. But why shouldn't they be, she had put ten whole pounds into their bowl on the table. But it seemed to please them a lot and they were raising their glasses a bit crookedly and saying Nancy Whiskey and things to her that they'd never have said otherwise.

There was no sign of Mrs Ryan; she had gone out again after her party piece. Nancy would like to have thanked her. Because now she had a lot of problems licked. And the great thing, the really great thing was this: it needn't cost a lot of money. In fact, if she was very careful it need cost hardly anything. She could take a lot of those glucose sweets and put them in a box, say, that could be a present for her mother one week. And she could give as presents those paperweights which she got from the drug companies – sometimes you could hardly see the name of the medicine they were advertising. And wasn't it just as well she had told nobody about the rise in her wages. She had negotiated it herself quietly, so no one need ever know about that at all.

Dee

They often had a drink on a Friday night in the pub beside the office. Dee would only stay for half an hour. The Lilac Bus wouldn't wait, she knew that. She knew too that a lot of people in the practice were surprised that she went home every weekend. It was so far, and there was so much to do in Dublin. Wasn't she very dutiful? Oh no, she had denied, no. It was selfishness: she went home because it was peaceful, there were no distractions, she could study at home. But the law books that crossed Ireland in her canvas bag came back again unopened as often as not. Dee Burke spent much of her weekends sitting at her bedroom window and staring out at Rathdoon. Until it was time to go back to Dublin again on Sunday evening.

And of course her parents were pleased. She could get off the bus at the corner and walk up to the golf club, waving cheerily as the Lilac Bus went on into town. For every Friday night in human memory Dr and Mrs Burke were at the golf club, and if there was a birth or a death or something untoward in between, people knew to phone the club and the Doctor would take the call.

They had been surprised at the beginning of the summer when she began to come home so regularly. Surprised but glad. It was great to have company round the house, and Dee was always the liveliest of the family. They would jump up with pleasure when she put her face around the door on a Friday night to join them and whoever else in the club bar.

Her father would get her a toasted sandwich and put his arm around her shoulder if she stood beside him at the bar counter. Her mother would smile over from the table. They were so delighted to have Dee home again. Sometimes her stomach rose and fell at their innocence and their kind welcome. What did people do when they didn't have the Burkes to go back to, Dee wondered? Went mad maybe? Went to discos? Got sense? Pulled themselves together? Oh, who knew what other people did? Who cared?

Tom Fitzgerald was quite handsome; she had never thought of it until tonight when he was laughing at her for flinging her own bag up on the roof rack. He had a lovely grin. He was an odd fellow – you could never get a straight answer out of him on anything. She knew nothing about him, nothing at all, and she had grown up fifty yards from him and his brothers. She didn't even know what he did for a living. She had asked her mother once.

"Don't you travel across the country sitting beside him? Why don't you ask him yourself?" her mother had said, not unreasonably.

"Oh, he's not the kind you could ask," Dee had said.

"Well then, you'll have to remain ignorant," her mother had laughed.

"At this stage of my life I'm not going to go into the drapery and ask personal questions to the Fitzgeralds about what occupation their son follows."

Nancy Morris was sitting in the bus, first as usual. She looked different somehow. Was it a new blouse or her hair? Dee wasn't sure – she wouldn't ask in case Nancy would start bewailing the cost of everything as she usually did. And yet she was getting a fine big salary, so Sam had told her. Far more than any of the receptionists or clerks were getting in the Solicitors' office. Maybe I won't sit beside her tonight, Dee resolved, but she knew she would. Who else knew Sam, who else could tell her about Sam Barry and his daily life except Nancy? Imagine being able to travel home with Sam's receptionist every weekend. It was like having a bit of

Sam with her. It took a lot of the loneliness away just to be able to talk about him. Even very indirectly, even if it meant talking about Mr Boring White and Mr Boring Charles as well. Because Nancy must never, never know that it was only Mr Sam Barry that she was interested in.

Nancy would talk for ever: she explained the routine and the kind of problems the consultants had, not being able to get beds quickly enough in the hospital, and all the complications of the Voluntary Health Insurance and the forms and people not understanding them. But she knew nothing about their lives outside the hospital. Nothing except what they told her and what the nurses told her, and that was little.

"Do their wives ever ring them at work?" Dee asked. It was like probing a sore tooth; she knew she shouldn't ask.

"Oh yes, sometimes they do." Nancy was maddening.

"And what do they say?"

"They're all very nice, they call me by my name."

That surprised Dee: Nancy was so unforthcoming and businesslike, you couldn't imagine anyone chatting to her.

"Oh yes, 'Hallo Miss Morris,' they say. All of them: Mrs White, Mrs Charles, Mrs Barry."

So that's what she meant by calling her by her name!

"And has Mrs Barry much of a Canadian accent?"

"Gosh, Dee, you do have a great memory for them all. No wonder you're so brainy and going to be a solicitor. Imagine you remembering she was a Canadian. No, not much of an accent, but you'd know she was from over there. American sounding."

Imagine my remembering she was Canadian? Imagine my being able to forget it! She doesn't know many people here ; she's far from home; it's not as if she grew up here and has her own circle of friends; she needs time to make a life for herself; we have to wait until things settle down.

Dee could never understand the logic of that. If they were going to wait until Candy Barry settled into Irish life they were building up more and more trouble for themselves. Why didn't they settle her back into Canadian life, she wanted to know? Before she had become isolated from her roots there. Why? Because of the children of course, the two little Barrys, small clones of their father, five and seven. He wasn't going to let those go four and a half thousand miles away and see them once a year on a visit.

But what about the children that he and Dee would have together? That would be different. Wonderful but different. You didn't parcel away your two lovely sons because you were going to have a new family with somebody else. No indeed. Dee was immature to suggest it.

Sam used that word as a great insult. He said it had nothing to do with age. People younger than Dee could be mature and people much older than both of them would never achieve it. She didn't like the word, it seemed to mean whatever he wanted it to mean. Like when you're playing poker and the two is wild, the two can be any card you want it to be.

She didn't know why she asked Nancy about his work. She never learned anything new, but it was like seeing a photograph of some scene that you knew well; it was always interesting to see it again from another angle. The only bit she shouldn't have asked was about their wives ringing up. That had made her uneasy now.

Sam said that Candy never called him at work and yet Nancy Morris said she did. Nancy probably wanted to show off about how well she knew them all. Boasting. She was in the middle of some complicated diatribe about the telephone system now. Dee felt her eyes closing. She slept and dreamed that she was getting her parchment from the Chief Justice and Sam was there congratulating her, and a photographer from the *Evening Press* had the three of them lined up and was writing their names down in his notebook.

Dee often dreamed that Sam was part of her life: she felt that this must signify that she was not guilty about him and that everything they had together was above board and out in the open. Not too much out in the open of course, but not hole-in-the-corner either. For example, her flat-mate Aideen knew all about Sam, and met him when he called. And Sam's friend Tom knew too: he used to go out to meals with them sometimes. So it wasn't as furtive as you might think. Sam had wanted to know why her parents didn't cop on, but Dee had said it would never cross their minds, and anyway she was softening them up for the future by insisting she had no romantic interests yet but would certainly fall for somebody highly unsuitable when the time came. Dee had pealed with laughter over this, and Sam had looked sad. She had stopped laughing suddenly and he had been very quiet.

"The future mightn't be perfect," he said. "Not for us: you shouldn't hope too much, you know."

"The future's not going to be perfect for most people," she had said cheerfully. "But they have to keep hoping, otherwise what's the point of anything?"

That had seemed to cheer him a little, but he had been quieter than usual.

Dee wasn't sure why she came home so often now. Aideen couldn't understand it either.

"Sure if you're down there, he'll never see you. Can't he ring you here, if he has a free minute?"

True. But he was having less and less free minutes. Candy's parents were over from Toronto. They had to be shown round. One of the little blonde boys had fallen off a bicycle and opened his forehead; he had to be visited in hospital, and looked after when he got home.

There was the family holiday on the Shannon, on the cruiser, and the hurried phone calls from coinboxes when he was meant to be buying drinks or going to the Gents'.

And recently there were times that weren't explained at all, but they were times that seemed to have no minutes in them all the same. It was easier in Rathdoon, he *couldn't* ring her there, even if he wanted to. Her father would recognise his name, the phone was in the hall, it would be hopeless. Perhaps that's why she went, because anything was better than sitting in a place where he could ring and didn't.

Aideen said she should fight harder for him, force him to leave that Candy. He had been so keen on Dee at the start that he would have done anything for her; now she had let him believe that he could have it both ways. But Dee thought she might want it both ways too. She didn't want a huge scandal, and having to leave her apprenticeship and end up half-qualified, half-married, half-home-wrecker and half-disgraced. Aideen said that was nonsense and that Dee's parents had been able to accept that her brother was living with a girl, so why couldn't they accept what she planned to do. Dee thought there was a lot of difference between Fergal living with his girlfriend when everyone knew that they would get married soon anyway, and her making off with a well known Dublin consultant and forcing him to abandon his wife and two little boys. It was a matter of degree. Aideen had said that was nonsense, it was all Sin and it was all not Respectable. So why not do it?

Why not? It wasn't really up to her any more: Sam was not nearly so ardent. In fact once or twice he had made excuses that seemed just like the things he had said to Candy on the phone a year ago. "Sorry love, I tried, but it's useless, there's this meeting, it's the only time they can get all the people together. I pulled out last time. I can't be seen to do it again." Very familiar. Frighteningly familiar. But was he making excuses to his young mistress so that he could be with his middle-aged Canadian wife? Or was there another young mistress? Someone even younger than twenty-three? Someone who didn't sigh and groan when he cancelled an arrangement? Someone who never suggested that Candy be sent back to Toronto?

Dee was remarkably calm about the possibility of a rival. She couldn't take it seriously. He really *was* a busy man, by anyone's standards; he worked long hours and there were still more people straining to see him. He had barely time for one relationship, not to mention two. To think of three would be ridiculous. Nobody could juggle that many romances and promises and endearments in the air. Nobody.

She was glad when they stopped, just for the chance to stretch her legs. Tom gave them ten minutes and not a minute more in the pub beside the garage where he filled up the Lilac Bus. The men usually had a half-pint each and sometimes Dee bought Nancy a gin and orange and Celia a bottle of Guinness. She would have a little brandy herself if her stomach felt cold and nervous. But tonight she felt all right. Sam was away on his conference.

He had rung her from the airport to say goodbye. He had said he loved her and that he'd see her on Monday night, late when he got back from London. He'd tell Candy the conference went on until Tuesday. That was fine, it was ages since he had been able to stay a full night, she would make sure that there'd be no confrontation and scenes. Just like it had been in the beginning.

They were settling back in the bus. Poor Mikey Burns, the bank porter, who was so nice apart from all his lavatory jokes, said that he felt much better now that he'd shaken hands with the wife's best friend. He said it twice in case people hadn't got it. Kev Kennedy still hadn't.

"You're not married, Mikey," he had said.

Mikey looked defeated.

Dee said she mustn't sleep too much on the bus, it gave her a cramp in her shoulders, and Nancy said there was a great way of getting rid of tension in the neck you had to hang your head down as if it was a great weight and then roll it around. Judy Hickey joined in the conversation unexpectedly and said that this was one of the principles of yoga and seemed greatly in agreement. Dee thought Nancy was put out by this, as if she didn't want to join up with yoga over anything.

He would be in London now, staying in that big posh hotel near the American Embassy where she had once spent a weekend with him as Mrs Barry. It had been so racy, and she kept thinking she'd meet someone from home as if anyone from Rathdoon would ever go inside a place like that. He had said there would be a reception at 8.30 and they would all wear name badges. It would have begun now. She felt an urge to talk about him again. This would be her last chance since she wouldn't be able to mention him at home.

"I expect they go away a lot on conferences, professional sort of things," she said to Nancy.

"Sometimes." Nancy was vague. "Not often. Of course they've all had their holidays in August, and you've no idea how hard it is to fix appointments; people don't understand that doctors, specialists, have to have holidays like anyone else. More than anyone else," she added righteously.

Dee wasn't going to go down that martyr road; she wanted to hear about Mr Barry being invited to this very prestigious gathering in London. She wanted to hear what he said when he got the invitation, and she wanted to hear Nancy say that he was coming back on Tuesday, so she could hug that to herself like a little secret.

"Yes, but didn't you say one of them was off to a conference this weekend?" she said.

"No." Nancy was puzzled. "No, definitely not."

"Maybe they'd go and not tell you?" Dee's heart had started to move in a very unacceptable rhythm.

"I don't think so," Nancy was lofty. "But anyway it wouldn't be this weekend, because I know where they're all going, as it happens. It's a big do. Mr and Mrs Barry – she's a Canadian you know – well, they're having their tenth wedding anniversary party tomorrow, and it's going to be a big barbecue. Mr Barry asked me to pray specially that it wouldn't rain."

She didn't hear anything else for the rest of the journey home. But she must have managed to nod or smile or something because she certainly didn't notice Nancy looking at her puzzled or anything. She felt as if somebody had opened her throat just under the gold horseshoe he had bought her as a pendant that time in London, and poured in a jug of iced water. The water was freezing up again. Why? That was all she wanted to know. Why the elaborate lies? Filled with such detail, about the name badges, the names of Americans and French and Germans that he was going to meet? Did these people exist at all, or had he picked names out of a phone book or out of literature? Why? If he and his wife had such a good marriage that they were gloating publicly with a big babyish barbecue over the whole thing . . . then why did he need Dee as well?

She went over it all, from the very start, when they had met at a party on the day of a Rugby International. It had been a big lunch where people had been invited to pre-match snacks and most people had such a good time they had stayed on and watched the match on telly instead. Dee had felt guilty about their tickets and all the young disappointed hopefuls who could have used them and Sam had gathered up half a dozen and run out on the road and given them to the first crowd of passers-by he saw. They had looked through the window and laughed at the waving kids and the eager way they had run towards Lansdowne Road. She and Sam had laughed a lot that afternoon, Candy was at the other end of the room talking about recipes. When they were leaving, Sam had said, "I must see you again," and she had laughed a peal of delight, and told him it was pure Hollywood.

"I am pure Hollywood," Sam had said, and somehow it had sounded endearing and nice. She had given him work and home numbers and he had called the next day. He had pursued her, yes, that wasn't too strong a word for it. *Pursued*. She had said she didn't want to get involved with a married man, and he said that he knew it was more pure Hollywood and pure corn and pure things-that-married-men-said, but actually his marriage was empty and a great mistake and something he should never have done but he had been in Canada and lonely and far from home; and that, apart from Dee altogether, he and Candy would undoubtedly drift their separate ways when the children were old enough to understand, and that he would be very gentle and careful, and that he would love her always. Now why would someone do that? If you loved one person and thought they were smashing and lovely and fresh why would you then have big parties and hand-holding and a lot of bullshit with another person? What was the point? Or suppose you loved the other person and enjoyed being married to her for ten years and adored the two little boys and everything then why would you tell lies about being fresh and lovely and tell tall tales about conferences in London with name badges to someone else? It was beyond understanding, and Dee felt that something in her head was about to break with the effort of understanding. She bent forward a little. Tom's eyes in the mirror caught the movement.

"Are you OK Dee?" he called.

"Sure," she muttered.

"Right, coming to your corner in five minutes," he said. He must have thought she was car-sick.

"We're never home already?" She was genuinely shocked. She thought they were seventy miles from Rathdoon. "You should try driving Concorde," she said, managing a sort of joke for him.

"Sure that would be child's play after the Lilac Bus," Tom grinned back at her.

She wondered should she go straight home and not get off at the golf club. But that would be worse, back to an empty house on her own. No, better join in and be with people who would talk and laugh and be pleased to see her.

She opened her bag and got out a mirror before she went in. Unbelievably she was not too bad, her face tanned from all those weekends at home, her hair straight and shoulder length – Sam said it was like an advertisement for shampoo, which was high praise. Her eyes normal looking, not wild. No, she wouldn't frighten her parents and their friends. In she would go and when they asked her what she'd have she'd say she had a stomach upset and could she have a brandy and port. Someone told her once that this was a great drink and it cured every ill. Or most ills anyway.

They were delighted to see her as always, but they were bursting with news. They couldn't wait for the drink to be in her hand so that they could drink a toast. They had had a phone call from Fergal – what do you think, he and Kate had bought the ring, they were getting married just before Christmas, wasn't it marvellous? And Kate's parents had been on the phone too and they had all said wasn't it wonderful the way things turned out, and maybe young people nowadays were much wiser than their parents and didn't rush into things. Dee Burke raised her glass of port and brandy and drank the health of her brother Fergal and her new sister-in-law-to-be, Kate, and she wondered with her mother what they both would wear to the wedding. And the drink went down through that channel where there had been iced water before, and it sort of burned it with a fiery anaesthetic and she began to think that whoever said it cured all ills might have had a point.

But it didn't bring sleep. And she had to move gently if she moved at all. The big old house was full of creaks and bumps. If you went to the lavatory during the night you woke the whole house. It was considered courteous to arrange your functions so that you didn't have to. Her parents talked on long downstairs. They had been married for thirty years, she realised. They never made much of anniversaries and when her mother was fifty last year it had been very politely ignored. No showy barbecues for them, no public displays.

But that didn't matter. What was she going to do? Was she going to pretend that she knew nothing, let him lie on about London? No, that would be living out a total dishonesty. But then wasn't he prepared to do that with her? Some of the time. And with Candy some of the time. He didn't have this high regard for total honesty. How had he not known that Nancy would prattle about it? She had told him that she travelled home on the same minibus every weekend as his receptionist. But Sam didn't know that she talked to Nancy about the consultants, and Sam would never believe for one moment that Nancy would mention something as trivial as his party to someone who was not meant to know him. Would she ring him at home and confront him? What earthly good would that do? None.

She would try to be calm and wait until daylight. What was that thing you were meant to do to your neck and shoulders? She tried what she remembered of the instructions but it just made her feel worse.

An hour later she understood what insomnia was about. She had never understood why people didn't just turn on the light and read if they couldn't go to sleep.

Another hour later she laughed mirthlessly to herself about her lack of sleeping pills. There she was, a doctor's daughter, and another doctor's lover and she hadn't one little Mogadon to call her own. A bit after that she started to cry and she cried until she fell asleep at twenty to eight just as her mother was creaking down the stairs to put on the coffee.

She woke after one o'clock: her mother was standing by the bed.

"Is your tummy better?"

Dee had forgotten the so-called gastric attack to excuse the ports and brandy.

"I think so," she said bewildered.

"If you're well enough, can you do me a favour? We've had another phone call from Fergal," her mother paused expectantly.

"The wedding's off?", Dee said rubbing her eyes.

"No, stupid, but they're coming this evening, about six o'clock. Can you run me into town, I'll want to get things."

"Into town" meant the big town seventeen miles away. "Down town" meant Rathdoon itself.

46

"What do we want to go into town for?"

"You can't get anything nice here, anything different."

"Mummy, in the name of God, isn't it only Fergal? Why do we want anything *nice*, anything *different* for Fergal?"

"But it's Kate as well."

"But hasn't he been living with Kate for a year? Are you losing your marbles or something, what would she want anything nice and different for? Can't we go to Kennedy's and get some ham or lamb or whatever we'd be having anyway?"

"Well if you don't want to drive me, you need only say so. I'm sure your father won't mind giving me a quick spin into town," her mother was huffy now and annoyed.

"It's not a quick spin, you know it, it's seventeen miles. It's a bad road, it's jam packed with shoppers on a Saturday in there, we'll never get a parking place, the whole thing will take three hours."

"Well, don't *you* worry about it, Madam: you're so busy you can sleep on into the broad daylight – I see what a demanding life *you* have. No, your father may be able to give up his one game of golf a week to take me."

Dee got out of bed, and picked up a dressing gown.

"I'll have a bath and I'll take you now, but I want you to know that there's a grave danger you're going mad. Next week you'll be going into town to get something nice and unusual for me."

"If you were bringing home a fiancé I'd be glad to," her mother said. "And by the way, do you never wear pyjamas or a nightdress or anything? Isn't it very peculiar to wear nothing at all in bed?"

"It's very peculiar Mummy – I'd say I'd be locked up if anyone knew."

"Oh there's nothing like a smart aleck, nothing as lovely as your own daughter turning into a smart aleck," said her mother and went downstairs happily to make a list.

Mrs Burke bought a new tablecloth and six napkins to

match. Dee cast her eyes to heaven so often her mother asked her not come into the next shop to be making a show of her. She was moved on three times by guards, hot harassed men who could never have dreamed that this is what it would be like when they joined the force. She saw a woman slap her three-year-old hard on the legs until he roared in fright and his father thought she had gone too far and gave the woman a hard shove. Marriage! Dee thought. Family life. If a Martian were looking at us, he would think we must be insane to run towards it like a crowd of lemmings. And it's all we want, everywhere: romantic books, *Dallas* on the telly, everyone we know. Nobody seems to learn any lessons on the way.

Her mother came out weighed down with parcels just as a guard was coming at her again; she dragged the parcels and her mother into the car with one movement.

"You're becoming very rough Dee, very ill-mannered," Mother said, annoyed and flustered.

"It's all this naked sleeping," Dee said, smiling up at the guard. "That's the cause of it, I'm certain."

Half-way home Dee realised what had happened. That stupid Nancy had got the weekend wrong. That was it. Hadn't Sam said he'd be tied up with the family, *next* weekend. Imagine believing the daylight from Nancy Morris. She really was going mad, it wasn't just a joke she made to her mother, of course that was it. Nancy was fussing and filling in her appointment book and complaining about the cost of living and she hadn't heard.

The relief was immense: it was the joy of getting an exam, it was like going to confession, not that there had been much of that lately – it was like passing your driving test.

She laughed happily and her mother looked at her in alarm.

"Mummy, I was just thinking of the day I passed my driving test," she began.

"Well I don't know whether you'd pass it if you had it to do again," her mother said. "You've been hitting those potholes at a great rate, your father wouldn't like his car to be belted about like that."

"No, I was just thinking of the lovely feeling when the man said I passed. Would you like me to teach you to drive, Mummy, seriously?"

"I would not," her mother said. "And what's more I don't think I'll ever sit in a car with you again. Will you look at the *road*, Dee!"

"It's an open invitation. One lesson on a Saturday, one on a Sunday – sure you could drive us all to Fergal's wedding."

She felt light-headed and happy. If she saw stupid Miss Mouse as Tom called her, she would have mown her down.

When Fergal and Kate arrived, Dee thought they both looked slightly touched. They were a revolting mixture of over-talkativeness and utter wordlessness. They explained at tedious length how they had become mature in the last few months and both of them had developed this sense of their immaturity and lack of responsibility at exactly the same time. They wanted to make their commitment now in front of everyone, rather than shilly-shallying any longer. Doctor Burke, who looked as if he wouldn't have minded if they never married, nodded and grunted appreciatively. Fergal's mother gasped and pounced on every word, and reminded them of every detail of John's wedding five years before, every detail that is except the one that his bride was four months pregnant. Dee switched off for a little and thought of Sam in London. He had said there would be papers all of Saturday afternoon but that he was going to skip the official dinner. Together they had looked at an English newspaper and circled plays or shows he might see. She wondered was it a nice warm night in London as it was here. Then it hit her like a tennis ball coming suddenly into her stomach. He had asked Nancy Morris to pray for a fine weekend for the barbecue. *This* weekend.

She wasn't able to eat the meringues which her mother had filled so carefully with a coffee flavoured cream to impress Fergal and Kate. She asked to be excused for a few minutes because she had remembered there was something she had to give Celia Ryan down in the pub.

"Won't it do later?" her mother had asked.

"No, she wants it now." Dee was standing up.

"Will I come down with you and have a pint?" She shooed Fergal away. "What a thought, after all this lovely meal Mummy's got for you. No, I'll be back in a few minutes."

"What does Celia want at this time of night?" Her father asked mildly. "Won't she be pulling pints and trying to help that poor mother of hers to cope?"

"See you," Dee called.

She ran up to her room for her handbag and swung down the road.

"Can you give me a pound of change for the phone, Celia?" she asked.

"God you're a great customer, if we had more like you we could open a singing lounge and have a cabaret on the profits," Celia laughed.

"Piss off, Celia. I'll have a brandy in a minute, I just want to make a call to Dublin."

Celia's level glance never changed, she never enquired whether the Burke phone was out of order, she just gave her the money.

"Could I get a call back in that box?" Dee wanted to know.

"Yes, I'll give you the number but I don't put it up – I don't want other people to know."

"You're a pal," Dee said.

"Barry residence," said the Canadian voice she hadn't heard since the one and only time she met its owner at that rugby party which was only a year and a half ago but felt like a lifetime.

"May I speak to Mr Sam Barry, please."

"Well, it's a little awkward just at this very minute. Who is this please?"

"It's Miss Morris, his receptionist."

"Oh Miss Morris, I didn't recognise your voice. I am sorry. Sam is just getting the barbecue going, it's a very delicate moment." There was a little laugh. "Once the thing has taken we can all relax. Can I ask him to call you, Miss Morris, I assume it's urgent?"

"I'm afraid it is, Mrs Barry." She sounded apologetic. "It's just a short message, but I should speak to him. It won't take a moment."

"Well, listen, I know he says that you are a rock of stability in a changing world, can I have him call you?"

"In the next half hour, if he could." Dee gave the number that Celia had written down.

"Rathdoon, what a pretty name!" Mrs Barry was determined to be charming to the rock of stability. Or else she was so happy about the anniversary barbecue she was at peace with the world. Dee didn't wait to find out.

"Very pretty. Bye, Mrs Barry." She hung up; she was shaking. She sat on a stool at the bar. Celia made it a large brandy but charged only for a small one. Dee made a move to protest.

"Nonsense, you're always buying me drinks."

"Thanks." She held the glass with both hands. Celia must have noticed the shake.

"They tell me your Fergal's engaged," Celia said.

"Lord, that didn't take long." Dee grinned.

"Oh, it's stale news, I heard last night when I came off the bus."

"So did I: the parents are over the moon."

"Well, they don't have to pay for the wedding," Celia laughed.

"Celia, stop that, you sound like Nancy Morris."

The phone rang. Celia refilled her glass wordlessly and Dee slipped into the booth.

"Hallo," she said.

"A call for you," exchange said.

"Miss Morris?" Sam asked.

"No, Miss Burke," Dee said.

"What?"

"Miss Burke speaking, can I help you?"

He wasn't sure. "I'm sorry, I was asked to ring a Miss Morris at this number . . . "

"No, you weren't, you were asked to come in from the barbecue and talk to your mistress Miss Dee Burke. That was the message I gave your wife."

"DEE. DEE." He was horrified. There was actual fear in his voice.

"Oh, she was very nice about it, she got a pencil from her purse and wrote down the number. She said Rathdoon sounded a pretty place."

"Dee, what are you doing?" His voice was a whisper.

"I'm at home for the weekend, like I told you I would be. The question is, what are YOU doing. Did they cancel the conference? Let's see, you were leaving the airport about four thirty – gosh, did they tell you at London airport or did you have to get into town?"

"Dee, I can explain exactly what happened but not here and now; what did you really say to Candy?"

"Oh just that, and she really did say that Rathdoon sounded pretty – ask her."

"You didn't . . . but why?"

"Because I felt it was all so confusing, all this business of lies and saying one thing and everyone knowing it wasn't true. Everyone. I thought it would be easier not having to pretend so much."

"But . . . "

"I mean she knows, Candy does, that you'll be spending Monday night with me, and so now you don't have to lie to her about that, and I know that you and Candy are having a marvellous tenth anniversary barbecue and that Mr Charles is there and Mr White and all your friends and they were all watching you start up the fire. She told me all that, so

52

there's no more pretending: it will be much easier from now on."

"You didn't, Dee. You didn't really say those things to Candy."

Her voice was very hard now. Very hard. "You'll have to find out now, won't you."

"But she said it was Miss Morris on the phone."

"Oh, I told her to say that." Dee sounded as if she were explaining things to a child. "Much simpler for your guests; I mean I don't know what you want to tell other people, but we'll talk about it all on Monday, won't we?"

"Dee, please don't go, you've got to explain."

"I have explained."

"I'll ring you back."

"Ring all you like, this is a pub."

"Where are you going now?"

"I see the real Miss Morris over here in a corner. I think I'll buy her a gin and orange and tell her all about us. That will make it easier for me to ring you at work; you see, I couldn't before because she knew me, but now with all this new honesty . . . "

"What new honesty?"

"What Candy and I have been talking about."

"You're a bitch, you told Candy nothing; this is a game, some vicious little game."

"Hush hush, don't let them hear you."

"Where will you be tomorrow?"

"I'll see you on Monday night, as arranged: come any time, straight from work if you like now that there's no need to hide things any more."

"I beg you, tell me what you told Candy."

"No, YOU must ask Candy that."

"But if you told her nothing then . . . "

"That's right, you'll have walked yourself into it."

"Dee."

"Monday."

"I'm not going to be blackmailed into coming round to

you on Monday."

"Suit yourself. I'll be at home then, if I don't get called away or anything." She hung up.

"If he rings again, Celia, will you say you never heard of me and I haven't been in all night?"

"Sure," said Celia.

She went back to the house. Fergal was explaining that there came a time in your life when you couldn't play any more – you had to face up to things.

"Jesus Mary and Joseph, Fergal, you should have been a philosopher!" Dee said admiringly.

"Did you have a drink with Celia Ryan?"

"I had two large brandies, mother dear," Dee said.

"How much was that?" Fergal the man saving for a mortgage was interested now in the cost of fun.

"I don't know; I only paid for one small one when I come to think of it." There were sudden tears in her eyes.

"Dee, why don't you and I go for a walk for a bit and let the wedding talk go on to a crescendo here?" Doctor Burke had his blackthorn stick in his hand.

They walked in silence. Down past the chip shop and over the bridge and on to the fork in the road.

It was only coming back that there was any chat.

"I'll be all right, Dad," she said.

"Sure I know you will, aren't you a great big girl and won't you be a solicitor one day, a fierce terror making them all shake in the district court?"

"Maybe."

"Of course you will, and all this other stuff will sort itself out."

"Do you know about him?" She was genuinely surprised.

"This is Ireland, child. I'm a doctor, he's a doctor, well a sort of one – when they get to that level it's hard to know."

"How did you hear?"

"Somebody saw you and thought I should know, I think,

a long time ago."

"It's over now."

"It may be for a while . . . ."

"Oh no it is, tonight."

"Why so suddenly?"

"He's a liar and nothing else; he lied to her and to me – why do people do that?"

"Because they see themselves as having lost out and they want some of everything, and society doesn't let us have that so we have to tell lies. And in a funny way the secrecy keeps it all going and makes it more exciting at the start."

"You know what it's like all right; I don't know how you could."

"Oh, the same way as your fellow does."

"DADDY. No, not you. I don't believe it."

"Oh years and years ago. You were only a toddler."

"Did Mummy know?"

"I don't think so. I hope not. But she never said anyway."

"And what happened to the girl?"

"Oh she's fine; she hated me for a bit, that was the worst part – if she had been just a little bit understanding. Just a small bit."

"But why should she?" Dee was indignant.

"Why, because she was young and lovely like you are and she had the world before her, and I had made my way and it was nice but a bit, you know . . . a bit samey."

"She should have shook your hand like a chap and said 'No hard feelings, Johnny Burke, you'll be a treasured memory'," Dee was scathing.

"Something like that," her father laughed.

"Maybe she should have." Dee linked her father companionably. "Because you're a much nicer man than Sam Barry will ever be. I think he deserves a bit of roasting, actually."

"Ah well, roast away," her father said goodnaturedly.

"You've never listened to me up to now – there's no reason why you should now."

Dee sat in her room and looked down at the town. She thought she saw Nancy Morris sitting on the wall near the chip shop, but decided that it couldn't be. Nancy . . . pay for a whole portion of chips . . . ridiculous.

Mikey

Mikey always said that you couldn't come across a nicer crowd of girls than the ones who worked in the bank. The men were grand fellows too but they were often busy with their careers and they wouldn't have all that time to talk. And one of the men, a young buck who'd be some kind of a high manager before he was thirty had taken it upon himself to say to Mikey that it would be appreciated if he watched his sense of humour since the bank ladies had found it rather coarse on occasions. Mikey had been very embarrassed and had said nothing all day. So silent was he that the nice Anna Kelly who was pure gold asked him if he felt all right. He had told her what the young buck said, and Anna Kelly had said that banks were stuffy old places and maybe the buck had a point: jokes were fine with friends, but God the bank, it wouldn't know how to laugh if you were tickling its funny bone for a year.

So he understood now and he never uttered a pleasantry within the bank walls again. If he met them on the street that was different; he could pass a remark or make a joke like anyone then because they were all on neutral ground. And he used to tell the girls about his family in Rathdoon, well, about the family that Billy and Mary had really. The twins with the red hairs and the freckles and then Gretta with the pigtails and the baby, a big roll of butter with a laugh you could hear half a mile away. He told Anna Kelly that sometimes on the summer evenings when it would be very bright the twins wouldn't have gone to bed, and they'd be sitting at their window waiting till the Lilac Bus turned into the street and Uncle Mikey would get off. They collected stamps and badges, any kind of badges, and he had them all on the lookout for anything of that order so as he never went home empty-handed.

He was the only one of the bank porters who came from the country. The rest were all Dubliners: they used to laugh at him and say there'd have to be an official enquiry as to how he got the job. But they were a very good-natured lot, and there was great chat all day as they manned the doors, or wheeled the big boxes on trolleys where and when more money was needed or had to be put away. They delivered letters and documents up and down the street. They knew a lot of the customers by name and they got great Christmas presents altogether.

The Lilac Bus had started just when Mikey had needed it. His father was getting senile now, and it was hard on poor Billy and Mary to have the whole business of looking after him. But it would have been a long way to come back without Tom FitzGerald and the little minibus that dropped you at the door. Imagine having to get yourself to the town by a crowded train, packed on a Friday night and maybe not a seat, and then after that to try and organise the seventeen miles home. It would take all day and all night and you'd be exhausted.

His old father was pleased to see him sometimes, but other times the old man didn't seem to know who he was. Mikey would take his turn spooning the food, and combing the matted hair. He would play the Souza marches his father liked on the record player, and put the dirty clothes in the big buckets of Dettol and water out in the back. Mary, who was Billy's wife and a sort of a saint, said that there was no problem to it if you thought of it all as children's nappies. Into a bucket of disinfectant for a while, throw that out, into a bucket of water a while and throw that out and then wash them. Weren't they lucky to have space out the back and a tap and a drain and all. It would be desperate altogether for people who lived in a flat, say.

And the nurse came twice a week and she was very good too. She even said once to Mikey that he needn't come back *every* weekend, it was above the call of duty. But Mikey had said he couldn't leave it all to Billy and Mary, it wasn't fair. "But they'd be getting the house: what would Mikey be getting?" the nurse had pointed out. Mikey said that sort of thing didn't come into it. And anyway, wasn't it a grand thing to come back to your own place.

The twins told Mikey that there was never any fighting when he came home and Mikey was surprised.
    "Why would there be fighting in this house?" he asked.
    The twins shrugged. Phil and Paddy were afraid of being disloyal.
    "Sure you couldn't be fighting with your poor old grandfather, he would never harm the hair of your heads," Mikey said.
    The twins agreed and the matter was dropped.

    They loved Mikey around the house and he had a fund of jokes for them. Not risky ones of course, but ones they could tell anyone. Gretta even wrote them down sometimes so that she'd remember them to tell them in class. Mikey never told the same one twice; they told him he should be on the television telling them one after another with a studio audience. Mikey loved the notion of it. He had once hoped that he might be asked to do a turn for the bank's revue but nobody had suggested it, and when he had whispered it to that nice Anna Kelly, she said she had heard that you had to be a member of the union to be invited, that only members of the IBOA were allowed to perform. He had been pleased to know that, because otherwise he would have felt they were passing him over.

He had his doubts about the Lilac Bus when he arrived the very first Friday. Tom Fitzgerald had asked them to be sure not to wave any money at him, because the legalities of the whole thing were what you might call a grey area. He did have the proper insurance and everything, and the Lilac Bus had a passenger service vehicle licence, but there was no point in courting disaster. Let them all give him the money when they were home in Rathdoon where it would be nice and calm. None of them had understood the ins and outs of it but they all agreed. Mikey wondered if people like Doctor Burke's daughter and Mr Green's son Rupert would fancy sharing a journey home with Mikey Burns the bank porter and the son of poor Joey Burns who before he lost his wits had been a great man for standing waiting till Ryan's pub opened and nothing much else. But Dee and Rupert were the salt of the earth, it turned out. There wasn't an ounce of snobbery between the pair of them. And Mrs Hickey, she was a lady too but she always seemed pleased to see him. Nancy Morris was the same as she always had been since she was a schoolgirl, awkward and self-conscious. Nothing would get her out of that, she'd be an old maid yet. Celia Ryan was another fish altogether: it was a mystery she hadn't married someone by now. She always looked as if her mind was far away, yet she was meant to be a powerful nurse. He knew a man who'd been in Celia's ward, and he couldn't speak highly enough of her. He said she was like a legend in the hospital.

Nowadays he enjoyed the journey home, after he had got over his shyness of the first few runs. He would tell them a joke or two; they weren't a great audience, not like Gretta and Phil and Paddy, but they did smile and laugh a little and didn't it cheer them up?

Sometimes he sat beside Celia and he would tell her tales of the world of banking. He told her of all the new machines, and the days of bank inspections, and how the tourists would drive you mad, and how in the summer you'd have a line half a mile long of Spanish and French students all wanting to change about £1 each of their foreign money. Celia didn't tell many tales of the hospital, but she often gave him helpful advice about his own father, all in a low voice so that the others didn't hear her talking about incontinence pads and velcro fastenings for clothes.

But tonight it was the young Kennedy fellow sitting beside him. There was something seriously wrong with that boy. His brothers Bart and Eddie were the nicest fellows you could meet in a day's walk, but whatever had happened to young Kev he looked as if he had seen the Day of Judgement. You only had to address a civil word to him to have him leap out of his skin. Try to tell him a good story and he'd miss the point altogether. Mikey thought he'd teach him a few tricks that might be of use to him, to be able to do a trick in a pub. But the young fellow looked at him with the two eyes staring out of his head and didn't take in a word of it. In the end Mikey let him be, staring out the window as if the goblins were going to leap out of the hedges and climb into the bus after him.

Mikey nodded off. It was easy to sleep in the bus. The two girls behind him were already asleep, dreaming of fellows probably. Mikey dreamed that his father was well and strong again and had opened some kind of import and export agency in Rathdoon and that he, Mikey, was the manager and that he was able to give grand summer jobs to Phil and Paddy and Gretta delivering letters to people up and down the street. He often dreamed of the children. But he never saw a wife for himself in the dream. Mikey Burns had missed the boat as far as wives were concerned. Too nervous and eejity at the time he should have been looking for one, and now at forty-five he wasn't the kind of forty-five year old that would be in the race at all. Better not make a fool of yourself going to dances or picking up fast-knowing women in pubs and being made to look thick altogether.

When they crossed the river and were really in the West they paused for the ten-minute comfort stop, and the half pint to open the throat a bit. Celia came up to him quietly and put an envelope into his hand.

"That's for the bedsores: it's all written on it, keep him moving as much as you can."

"Aw Celia you're terribly good, can I pay for this?"

"Are you mad Mikey? Do you think I paid for it? Dublin Health Authority would like you to have it as a little gift." They laughed. She was very nice.

What a pity he hadn't found a grand girl like Celia when he was young and promising looking. After all, he had a grand well-paid job now, he'd be able to make a home for anyone. The reason he didn't really have one wasn't money, it was lack of interest. He couldn't be buying a place and furnishing it and getting tables and chairs in it all for hmself. The room he rented was grand and comfortable and he denied himself nothing. He had a grand big telly and he had bought a mirror himself to fix to the front of the wardrobe the way he'd go out properly dressed. He had a lovely radio beside the bed which was a lamp and a clock and an alarm all in one. When he went out to people's houses, and the Dublin fellows often invited him up to their places, he was always able to bring a big box of chocolates, a fancy one with ribbon on it. He was able to give a good account of himself.

But when he'd been a young lad, who were they except the sons of poor Joey Burns and his mother had taken in washing and cleaned people's floors? It hadn't held Billy back: Billy strutted round Rathdoon as if he owned it, as if he were as good as any other citizen of the place. And wasn't he right? Look where he was now, he had all kinds of business interests, he employed five people in Rathdoon. He had the take away shop; nobody believed there was a need for it until it appeared. Half the families in the place ate Billy's chicken and chips on a Saturday night, and they had fried fish too, and hamburgers. And they sold cans of lemonade, and stayed open late to get the crowds going home from Ryan's, and Billy had put up two huge mesh litter bins at his own expense and everyone was delighted with him.

And he had an insurance business as well. Not a big one but anyone who wanted cover went through him – it could all be filled in quickly in the house. And he had some kind of a connection with a fellow who came to do tarmacadaming. If you wanted the front of a place all smartened up then Billy would get other people with their places facing the same way to agree and the man with the machine and the tar would come and it was cheaper for everyone, and the place looked a king to what it looked before. A whole section of the main street looked really smart now, and Billy had got a tree planted in a tub and it was like something you'd see in a film. Billy had the brains and Billy never ran away the way Mikey ran off up to Dublin after his mother had died. Billy had stayed to marry Mary Moran who was way beyond anyone they'd ever have thought about. Or that Mikey would have thought about.

He was looking forward to being home tonight. He had a computer game for the twins' birthday. It was several cuts above the Space Invaders they had tried out once, and it could be plugged into any kind of television; he had been playing it on his own television all week but the shop assistant said it would work as well on a smaller set. The twins had their birthday on Monday and he was going to give them the game on Sunday afternoon. He would set up the room with the curtains pulled and pretend they were going to watch something on the television, and then would come the surprise. He had got a smart red girl's handbag for Gretta, even though it wasn't her birthday, because he didn't want her to be left out, and a yellow rabbit for the baby in case it might have feelings of discontent in its pram.

Mary would never let him near his father on the Friday night, she'd have a supper warm for him, or if it had been a busy day she'd run across the road to the family take away and get him fish and chips as soon as she saw the Lilac Bus pull up. She used to thank him so much for coming back to help with his father, and she'd tell him funny things about the children and what they had done during the week. They were back at school now so there would be tales of what divilment Phil had got up to and the threatening messages that came home about him from the Brothers.

Mikey was the second to get out. They would leave Doctor Burke's daughter up at the golf club entrance; her parents were always there of a Friday night and she'd go and join them. Then when it came to the end of the street the first drop was Mikey. He would take down Nancy Morris's huge suitcase which weighed as light as a feather and leave it inside the bus because she and Kev Kennedy would be next out, and Kev had nothing with him ever except a parcel which he kept under his seat.

Mikey advised them all to be good and if they couldn't they should be clever and if they couldn't be clever then they should buy a pram. He laughed happily and closed the door behind him.

There was no light in the kitchen and no meal on the table. There was no sign of Mary and no note either. He didn't mind not seeing Billy – his brother was usually up at the take away or in Ryan's doing some deal with someone. But Mary?

He looked in the other rooms. His father was asleep, mouth open, wheelchair near the bed, on the chair a large chamber pot, optimistic since the old man was never able to time things so accurately.

There was a smell of disinfectant mixed with better smells. Mary had big bunches of flowers round the room. She always said that she thought it cheered the old man up, and sometimes she had seen him stretch out and touch the flowers gently. He snored lightly, there was a night light, and a Sacred Heart lamp as well.

Then he went up the stairs quietly. The twins had bunk beds; their toys and clothes and books were all around. Phil slept in a ball with his fists clenched; Paddy was more peaceful, lying on his side. Gretta looked funny with her long straight hair brushed out. He remembered her with plaits for as long as she had been old enough to force her hair into them. She had a smile as if she was dreaming. She was a thin little thing, gawky and plain-looking but she had a smile that would tear the heart out of you. Even when she was asleep.

The door of Billy and Mary's bedroom was open: they weren't there. The baby round and soft like a cream bun lay in its cot near the bed. There was a lovely white lacy bedspread, and on the wall there was a picture of Our Lady in a field of flowers. It had a blue lamp lighting under it. It was called "Queen of the May". Mary told Mikey once that the day she and Billy got engaged he had won a competition at a carnival where you had to throw rings over things and he had chosen that picture for her because she liked it so much.

Mikey put his small bag in his own room which was neat as anything. She always had a bright clean pillowslip on the top as if he was the highest quality coming for the weekend. Sometimes Mikey's mind went back to what the house had looked like in his mother's day when they hadn't any such style or time for it.

It was puzzling, but maybe she had gone to get him fish and chips. He waited downstairs and listened to the news on the television. And eventually he began to get worried. They never left the children all alone in the house, even though they were perfectly safe, but it was just the way they were. His anxiety increased. He walked across to the take away and to his surprise there was Mary serving. There were four people waiting for their order and only one of the young girls who worked there was behind the counter. They were working flat out.

"Mikey, Lord is it that time already?" She was pleased but flustered to see him.

"Will I get behind there and give you a hand?" He knew the way he had done it with them a few Saturday nights during the summer when they had been very busy. And the prices were on the wall.

"Oh Mikey, would you?" She was very grateful.

He hung up his jacket and took an apron from a drawer. In a few moments they had the crowd thinned, and Mary was able to draw breath again. She spoke first to the girl who worked there.

"Treasa, would you take off your apron like a good child and run up to Ryan's. Tell them that we're short-staffed tonight and we'll be closing early. Tell them if they want anything to come down in the next half hour for it otherwise they'll be disappointed."

"Who will I tell, mam?" the child seemed worried.

"That's a point – not much use telling poor Mrs Ryan these days. Let me see, if there's anyone behind the bar helping, like Bart Kennedy, anyone like that, someone who looks in charge."

"Celia's home: she was on the bus, she'll probably have got behind the counter by now," Mikey said.

"That's it, tell Celia."

Treasa skipped off up the road, pleased to be out of the heat.

"Where's everyone?" Mikey looked around.

"Oh there's been a lot happening, I'll tell you all when we get back. Keep a brave face on it for half an hour more and then it will be done." A trickle of people came in, and Mikey served them, and just as Mary had guessed would happen a great influx came from Ryan's pub. They were full of good-natured abuse about it being against the law of the land to close the chipper before the pub. Mary had laughed good-naturedly and said wasn't she going above and beyond the call of duty to let them know now rather than have them going home with stomachs full of beer and nothing to soak it up.

She didn't want a portion for herself, so Mikey wrapped up his own choice, and when they had drained the fat, scrubbed the tops and swept up anything that could be swept up into black plastic bags which were tied with little wires at the top, they crossed the street and went home.

68

Mary heated a plate under the hot water tap, got out the tomato sauce and some bread and butter.

"Will I wet you tea or would you like a drop of anything?"

They got a bottle of Guinness each and sat down.

"Billy's gone. Gone for good."

He stared at her, fork half-way to his mouth.

"He went this day before lunch, he'll not be back. Ever."

"Ah no, Mary. That's not possible."

She took a sip of her drink and made a face.

"I never like the first sip, but it tastes grand after that." She smiled a weak little smile.

Mikey swallowed and said:

"It was just a bit of a row, that's all. People have rows, they get patched up."

"No, there was no row, there was no difference of opinion even."

Mikey remembered the way the twins had said there was no fighting when he was around the place.

"But just a bit of a barney now and then, these things sort themselves out, really they do." He was pleading now.

"No, I'll tell you it from start to finish – there was no row. Back there early on in the summer we did have rows all right: he was very touchy, I thought, bite the head off you as soon as look at you, but he said that's the way I was too. The children even noticed us."

"So what happened?"

"Well I don't know, honestly. But anyway we had a great summer, as you know, business was booming. He used to be tired but he was never cross any more, and what with the baby getting to be so grand – you know they're like divils for the first few weeks – anyway we hadn't a worry under the sun." She stopped and looked away beyond him.

Mikey was silent.

"Eat up your fish and chips, Mikey, you can eat and listen."

"I can't."

She lifted the plate from him and put it into the oven very low down. "You'll eat it later then. Today was when it all happened, and if I hadn't come back I wouldn't have known: I wouldn't have known at this moment. I wouldn't have known until the end of next week. And the whole of Rathdoon would have known before me."

"Known what, for God's sake?"

"He's gone off with Eileen Walsh, you know the one we said was too good to be working in a chipper. Well, she was far too good, she was only biding her time to go off with the owner of the chipper. That was the little plan. Could you beat it?" The voice was steady but the eyes were over bright.

"But it's only a fancy isn't it, it's a bit of madness. I mean where would they go, and what would they do? And how could he leave you and the baby and the whole family?"

"He's in love with her. That's the word: *In Love*. Isn't it marvellous? He was never *In* love with me; he loved me, of course, but that was different apparently."

Mikey stood up, but he didn't know what to do so he sat down again. Mary went on with the story.

"I was meant to be going into the town. There's always a lift in on Fridays and I had a list of things we needed for the take away, not things we get from the suppliers, but stupid things, big ashtrays for example and a couple of tins of bright red paint – we were going to paint the windows to match the geraniums, can you believe? But to go on with what happened: You know old Mrs Casey who's only just learned to drive, well she was giving me the lift and as soon as we were out on the road beyond the golf club, didn't the engine splutter and make these desperate sounds.

"Ah well, I said to myself, there's my day in town gone for its tea. But she's such a nice woman, Mrs Casey, you couldn't offend her. I told her it was a blessing in disguise and I could get the things next week and maybe I'd go home and make an apple tart since Mikey'd be coming back on the bus tonight."

A big lump came up in Mikey's throat.

"And I said to her to sit tight, I'd walk back and tell the Brennans in the garage to go out for her."

Mary took another sip.

"It was a gorgeous day, and I picked wild flowers from the hedges, and when I came in there was Billy at the table with a whole load of papers all round him. And I was delighted because he was meant to have been gone for the day. So I said wasn't this grand and we'd have a bit of lunch the two of us – something we hadn't done in years – and I saw that there was 'Dear Mary' on one piece of paper and on another and only two or three lines on each. And I *still* didn't know anything was wrong so I said 'Are you writing me love letters at my age?' as a kind of joke. You see I thought he was just back unexpectedly and was writing me a note to explain that he'd been in."

"Oh Mary, isn't this terrible," said Mikey, believing it for the first time since the saga had started.

"And this is the awful bit: he started to cry, he started to cry like a child. Well, I nearly dropped dead – Billy Burns crying. I ran to him to try and put my arms around him and he pushed me away. And he was sobbing like a baby that's getting teeth, so I said to him to hush it down or his father would hear. I'd left the baby next door but your father would have been having a doze and it would have frightened the daylight out of him like it was doing to me." She paused for a moment.

"Then he said about Eileen, and her expecting and all."

There was a silence and the clock ticked and the soft snoring sound of the old man could be heard from the back room.

"And he said he couldn't face me, and he was leaving a letter. And I said that he didn't have to go now, not at once, that surely he could stay and we could talk about what was to be done. But he said there'd been too much talking and that was it, now he was going." Mikey put out his big hand and patted Mary's arm hopelessly.

"And there was a lot of this and that, but funny no fight,

71

no shouts or me saying he was a bastard or him saying he couldn't bear me any more, that I was an old nag or anything."

"Well, no one could think that," Mikey cried loyally.

"No, he said I'd been the best wife and mother in the world, and that he couldn't tell me how sorry he was, he was just heartbroken, he said. All the papers were to show me that the chip shop is in my name, and the thousand pounds in the building society is for me, and the name of a solicitor who'd be able to find him, who'd pass letters on."

"And where does he think he's going?"

"To England. Where else?"

"And how will he earn a living for himself and this floosie?"

"She's not a floosie – Eileen a floosie? Billy would earn a living on the planet Mars, don't worry about that."

Mikey was struck dumb.

"But the thing that upset him most was his father, your father."

"Billy never gives much time to poor old Dad."

"No, but he thought it wasn't just for me to be left with him – to have to look after an old man who isn't my own father. I said that Da was the least of the problems, what I wanted to know was how he could leave me, his wife, his friend for years and years, for fourteen years married, and a year before that mad about each other. That's when he explained all this *In Love* business."

"What did you do?"

"What could I do? His mind was made up, he was leaving. He had a list of things he wanted me to do. There was a special sum of money left in one envelope that was for me to have driving lessons. I was to find out who taught Mrs Casey: whoever taught her could teach the divil himself. He was leaving the van. I was to ask Bart Kennedy to give me a hand and pay him a proper wage, I was to decide whether he should write to the children or not and what I should tell them, if anything. He thought I should say he had gone away for a bit and then they'd grow used to it."

Mary stood up to get another bottle of stout.

"He had been packing his things too, it nearly broke my heart to see his good shirts stuffed in all creased, and he had forgotten all his shoes. I asked him to say goodbye to your father – he's been very clear the past couple of days, knows all of us – but no, he wouldn't. I said he might never see him again and he said that he'd never see any of us again. That's when I got a bit frightened about it all. I knew there's never any changing his mind. So I decided I'd let him go, without screaming and roaring and begging."

"You let him walk out . . ."

"No, I said I'd go out and let him finish at his ease. I said he needn't bother about the letter now, he'd said it all, that I'd go out and get more flowers and things and keep out of his way for an hour or two until he left. That he could leave all the insurance papers where they could be found, and the solicitor who would pass on the messages to him if there was anything we hadn't thought of. He was SO relieved: you should have seen his face – you see he was afraid there'd be this big scene. He said that maybe I'd be glad of the change too, and I said, oh no, I wouldn't, I would miss him every day of the year and so would his children, and on the days when his father was clear his father would miss him too. I wasn't going to give him the nice comfortable feeling that he was doing us any favours. And out I went. I crept along the back way and he finished his packing and his leaving things out on the table, and your one came along in her car and he put the boxes and cases in and she kissed him just standing at our door and they drove off.

"When I came in it was all in neat piles on the table and a piece of paper saying 'Thank you very much, Mary. All the best, Billy.' So now you know everything, everything that's to be known."

"Isn't he a callous bastard, isn't he the biggest most selfish . . ."

"That won't bring him back."

73

"I'll bring him back, I'll get him back. He's not going to desert you, there's ways of bringing him back."

"Not if he doesn't want to come back! Will you have your fish and chips now, they'll go all hard otherwise?"

He hardly slept all night; it was only when the dawn came that he fell off and it wasn't long after that the twins were in the room followed by Gretta carrying a cup of tea. That was always their excuse to wake him: it was called bringing him his tea in bed. Most of it was in the saucer and some of it was on the stairs but it was still an excuse. They were full of plans for the day. They'd come down and wait while he was feeding grandpa and changing him: they accepted that routine as part of life like sunsets or having to wash your hands before meals. They wanted to show him a new game that had arrived in Brophy's shop. It was a huge thing like a Space Invaders but it cost twenty pence a time and they could only have three goes altogether unless of course Uncle Mikey wanted an extra game. And Mammy had said they could go on a picnic in the afternoon because since daddy was gone to Dublin for a bit there'd be no work to be done around the house and no one coming in about Insurance who had to have tea. And hadn't he better get up now in case all the good went out of the day.

Matty felt the day was very heavy on his hands, that things kept happening as if he were outside looking in at all the things that were happening instead of being part of them. He saw himself feeding his father slowly with a spoon, he saw himself cutting crusts off the sandwiches for the picnic, and climbing for the blackberries. It was like playing a part in a play.

He was glad when it was evening and the children went to bed; they went easily because he had promised them the most monstrous surprise of their lives tomorrow. Something that he absolutely guaranteed they would never expect. He assured Gretta that it was something she could share too and that there was a small non-birthday present for her as well.

"I don't know what I'd have done without you and that's the truth," Mary said. "The day just flew by for me." He was glad it had. He had arranged for two girls to help Treasa in the chip shop.

"Will Eileen not be in again?" Treasa complained. Her tone was guileless, she didn't know.

"No she won't, she's gone off somewhere; we'll get you these two young ones you've had in there before on bank holidays and high summer," he said firmly. "Mrs Billy and I are going to be down in Ryan's for a bit, so you'll know to send one of them down there if there's any problem, but a big bright girl like you, Treasa, you'll manage it. Don't you know it all like the back of your hand?"

Treasa was delighted with him.

"Oh go on, Mr Mikey, you and your Dublin chat" she said.

"Are we going off down to Ryan's?" he asked her.

He was going to make a joke and say something about stepping out together or hitting the high spots but he felt it would have been the wrong thing to do. She looked up at him, pleased and surprised that he seemed so eager.

"I'm not much company for you."

"I think we should go out though, don't you? From the start like. No hiding away in corners, no crawling out when people think you've got two heads. Be out there from the word 'go'. After all YOU haven't done anything."

"I've failed to hold onto my husband, that's a great crime around these parts."

"Oh I don't think so; aren't they all stuck into television every night here? I think you'd have to do far more than that to be a disgrace."

"I hate you to be involved in it, Mikey, you've been nothing but kindness itself, every weekend as nice as anything and look what happens to you: caught up in all the scandal, all the gossip."

"There won't *be* scandal and gossip, and that's up to you

to make sure of." He heard his own voice in his ears. He thought it sounded very confident, very sure. Mary must have thought so too.

"You're a great help to me taking all these decisions, I'm like one of those things in films that just walk about not knowing what they're at."

"Zombies," he said.

"Imagine you knowing that," Mary said.

"I see a lot of films," Mikey said. "What else have I to do?"

Ryan's was crowded. He put Mary in a corner and went up to the counter. Celia was going full strength and Bart Kennedy was giving her a hand. Mikey remembered his brother's instructions about paying Bart a proper wage and bile against Billy rose in his throat. To be able to calculate like that, to plan for her desertion, to deceive her so long.

"It's not like you to be short of a word, Mikey Burns." Celia was standing in front of him. She must have asked him his order and he hadn't heard.

"I'm sorry." He had to force his sense of outrage down before he could speak.

"Are you all right?" Celia's voice was concerned.

Mikey shook himself. He was full of brave words to his sister-in-law about how SHE was to behave, now he must do the same for himself. He could speak again, but he hadn't the heart for jokes.

He gave his order and carried the pint and the glass of Snowball across to Mary. As he was passing young Biddy Brady's engagement party, Nancy Morris of all people put her hand out as if to stop him. Wanted him to come and tell them some funny stories. And he always thought she was such a superior acting kind of a one, always looking in on herself and never having time for other people. Well, well.

"Not now, Nancy" he had said and he saw her face turning away embarrassed. He hadn't meant to be so short with her, but honestly, *now* of all times.

"Here we are" he said.

She had her head down looking at the floor.

"Look up Mary Burns, look up and smile."

She looked up and gave a watery smile.

"That's marvellous but it isn't a patch on your daughter's." She gave one of Gretta's sudden grins, the kind of grin that split a face in half; they both laughed.

"That's better," said Mikey, "now let's see what we'll do."

They got out a writing pad and made out a list of things she had to do this week. Ring suppliers – their names were all on some kinds of bits of paper on various spikes around the office. Billy Burns hadn't kept any books that would gladden the heart of a taxman but at least there was some method in his ways. They wrote out a kind of notice which she could give to anyone who called about insurance: "Mr Burns' policies are all being dealt with by the following office . . . " followed by the name of the solicitor's. She would give these to anyone with a laughing explanation that unfortunately as a mere woman she was never kept informed of the Master's doings. It seemed fairly sure that he hadn't absconded with other people's money, so his Book had been passed on or sold to some other agent by now. The solicitors would know. They listed the people they could call on to work in the take away, and how much they should be paid. He went for two further pints and two further Snowballs, and by that time they had covered every eventuality and worn themselves out.

"I'll sleep tonight, I'm that exhausted," Mary said, letting out that she hadn't slept the previous night.

"I'll sleep too: I'm less frightened," Mikey said. She looked at him gratefully: "You're very very good to me, but there's one thing you haven't mentioned at all."

"What's that?"

"What about you? Will you still be coming home on the

bus at weekends?"

"I'll get off the Lilac Bus before ten every Friday with the help of God," he said.

"You're very different tonight, you're not always cracking jokes and making games out of things people say. I find it much easier to talk to you, but hard to believe it IS you, do you know what I mean?"

"I think so" he said.

"Like I want to ask you do you want to come home to Rathdoon even more than at weekends, but I don't know how to put it. If I say, will you come back altogether, it looks as if I want you to come back and look after us all and take it all on, and that's NOT it. And then, if I don't ask you, you might get the notion you're not welcome."

"I've thought all that out too," Mikey Burns said.

"And what did you arrive at?" She leaned over the glass with its rim of froth. She couldn't wait to hear.

"You're still hoping in your heart he'll come back. That it's only a bit of summer madness. That it'll be all forgotten by the end of the month."

"I'd like it, but I don't think it's going to happen," she said simply.

"So, suppose I came home and settled myself in and Billy Boy came over the hill one fine day, where would that leave us all?"

"As we were, wouldn't it?" She looked at him enquiringly.

"No. I'd have to run away again, there wouldn't be room for us all in the one nest."

"So are you not coming back to us. I always thought you had a great soft spot for us altogether." She sounded sad.

"I'll come back for good if he isn't back for Christmas. That's the best way. That's the way to do it." He looked proud of his deductions.

"It's your home," she said gently. "You were always as welcome in it as the sun coming in the windows."

"You say that because you're like that. My brother Billy

78

didn't say it, did he, when he was leaving. He told you to get Bart Kennedy and pay him a proper wage."

"He did say it but I didn't repeat it. I didn't want to be making you think you had to do anything." She looked troubled now.

"What did he say?"

"He said . . . ah it doesn't matter what he said. He made it clear he thought of the place as your house too."

"I want to hear it."

"Why? What does it matter? We know he hardly knows what he's doing: he's half mad these days, he couldn't string words together."

"Well I'd like to know anyway, please," he said simply but firmly. This wasn't the giggling, jokey man of last weekend.

"He said something like: 'Mickey's not likely to settle down anywhere with anyone at his age, and he's very good to the old man, and the children love him. Maybe if he could find something for himself round here, he'd be in the place. Sure the house is half his anyway, he has a right to it.' It was something along those lines."

She didn't look at him, and he looked hard at the beermat which had a puzzle on it.

"Full of charm, my little brother, isn't he?"

"That's what he is: your little brother, don't ever forget that."

"And would it suit you, Mary, if I were to be about the place?"

"Would it suit me? Wouldn't I love it, isn't it what I always wanted? There's always been a living for us all in that take away alone, you've seen the takings, and if we were working in it together . . . "

"Well then, I'll come back at Christmas, that's the best. I might even get myself made redundant up at the bank, and have a lump sum. Those fellows up in the bank, the porters, are fierce organised, you'd never know what kind of a deal they'd get for me."

"And wouldn't it be dull for you, after Dublin?"

"No, don't I come home for nearly half the week as it is?"

"And maybe finding yourself a girl?" She was hesitant.

"I think brother Billy was right on that one, the time is past." He smiled an ordinary smile, not a screwed up one.

Rupert Green passed the table. "Did you see Judy Hickey at all?" he asked.

"No, I'm afraid we were talking, I didn't notice," Mary said.

"She could be round the corner behind the pillar there," Mikey pointed. Biddy Brady's party had linked arms and were singing "Sailing" and Celia's mother was arriving with a golf club as if she were about to brain them but as they all watched horrified it turned out that she had no such intention: she was about to join in the singing, and was in fact calling for one voice only, her own.

"I've met everyone from the Lilac Bus except the one I set out to meet," grumbled Rupert. "Dee Burke was just flying out the door, Miss Morris looks as if she's had a skinful, Kev is cowering in a corner, and the rest of the cast is at the counter canoodling."

"If she comes in what I'll tell her?"

"Oh I'll find her, I have to tell her something extraordinary."

Mary and Mikey looked politely interested.

He was gone.

"It's probably about some toadstool or mushroom; they're always talking about herbs and elderflowers and things," Mikey said. Mary laughed and tucked her bag under her arm.

"Won't you want another man?" he said suddenly. "I mean you're still young. Won't living with a brother-in-law cramp your style?"

"No," she said, "No, I won't. I mean, even if I could have one and I can't. But I think I'm through with all that sort of thing. I think I just want a bit of peace and for the children to be able to grow up happily enough and for me to have a place here, you know, just like you said, not running away. That will do me."

He remembered the dream that he had on the bus: the dream where there had been no wife but he was in charge of the children sending them on little messages up and down the street. He realised now there had been no Billy in the dream either. Some of the details were different, of course, but the central part was the same. He would be safe at home with them all. And there would be no demands made on him as a man. He could be just himself, and he'd be as welcome as the sun that came in the windows.

Judy

There had been four customers in the shop that afternoon, Judy had been taking note recently and writing it down in a little book. After lunch two students came in and spent almost half an hour reading books on herbalism and the art of home-made wines. An elderly man bought a copper bracelet for his arthritis and said that when the savages who came into his house and robbed him blind were leaving they pulled his copper arm band off in case it had been valuable. A woman with a tight hard face bought some Evening Primrose oil and asked could you dilute it with ordinary vegetable oil or baby lotion to make it go further.

It was a matter of weeks now before they had to close. Judy's heart was heavy as she walked toward the Lilac Bus. She was tired too, and not in form for a long drive to the West. She had been tempted to opt out. To go back to her little flat and have a long long bath listening to some nice music on the radio. Then to put on her caftan and her soft little slippers and lie there until the aches in her limbs and the build-up of a headache behind her eyes was gone. Fine advertisement I am for a health shop . . . she smiled to herself as she strode on towards the bus. Aching and creaking and bankrupt. No wonder people live such unhealthy lives if they see what good living leads to!

She hoped that Mikey Burns wouldn't be too loud tonight with his schoolboy jokes. He was a decent poor fellow but he was hard to take at any length. The trouble was that if you made no response to him he thought you hadn't heard and said it all again, and if you did manage a laugh he got encouraged and told you a few more.

She arrived just at the same time as Rupert: that was good, they could sit together in the back seat. It looked a bit standoffish if you were to keep a seat for anyone, but she really couldn't bear to be nudged by Mikey the whole way to Rathdoon or, even worse, to hear that solemn tedious little Nancy Morris telling her how to get free soap by buying toothpaste on a Wednesday or some such hare-brained scheme.

He was a good boy, Rupert: yes that was exactly how she would describe him if anyone asked her. Good. He was an only child of parents who were middle-aged when he was a toddler and who were old now that he was a man of twenty-five. His mother was sixty-seven and his father was seventy this year. But Rupert said there were no celebrations, his father was bedridden now and was failing by the week. Rupert said it was harder and harder each time he came home because he had this vision of his father as a hardy man with views of his own on everything, and then when he got into the big bedroom on a Friday night it was the same shock, the same readjustment – a paper-thin man with a head like a skull, with nothing alive except the big restless eyes.

Judy had known Rupert since he was a baby and yet she had only got to know him since the bus. He had always been a polite child. "Good morning, Mrs Hickey. Do you have anything for my pressed flower collection?" Protestants were like that, she had always thought in her good-natured generalisations: pressed flowers, politeness, neat haircuts, remembering people's names. Mrs Green was so proud of her Rupert, she used to find excuses to walk him down the town. The Greens had been married for twenty years when Rupert was born. Celia Ryan's mother in the pub had whispered that she gave Mrs Green a novena to St Anne that had never been known to fail, but because of her religion she had delayed using it. The moment she had said it, Catholic or no Catholic, St Anne had intervened and there you were, there was Rupert.

Judy told him that one night on the Lilac Bus and he laughed till the tears came down his face. "You'd better tell me about St Anne and what class of a saint she is. I suppose I should be thanking her that I'm here, or speaking sharply to her when times are bad."

Judy often smiled at Rupert's quaint ways. He was wonderful company and the same age as her own son, Andrew, miles away in the sun of California. But she could never talk to Andrew like she talked to Rupert – in fact she could never talk to Andrew at all over the years. That was the legal agreement.

Judy wondered would you recognise your own child.

Suppose she went to San Francisco now and walked through Union Square, would she immediately know Andrew and Jessica? Suppose they passed her by? They would be grown man and woman, imagine, twenty-five and twenty-three. But if she didn't know them and they didn't know her, what was all the point of giving birth and holding a child inside you for all that time? And suppose they did recognise her, that something like an instinct made them stop and look at this fifty-year old woman standing in the sunshine ... What would they do? Would they cry "Momma, Momma" and run to her arms like a Hollywood film? Or would they be embarrassed and wish she hadn't turned up? They might have their own idea of a momma back in Ireland. A momma who was just not suitable. That's what Jack said he would tell them. Their mother hadn't been able to look after them – no other details. And when they were old enough to hear details and understand them, they would be given Judy's address to write to and she could send them an explanation if she felt able to. She never felt able to because they never wrote. For years and years she had been rehearsing it and trying out new phrases, like practising for a job interview or a school essay.

Little by little she realised they were eighteen, nineteen, twenty. Well old enough to ask about an unsuitable mother. Well old enough to be told. But no request ever came.

She didn't even write to Jack's brother after a while. Jack's kind big brother who had given them all a home on the West Coast of America but who had always tried to patch up the split. He had told her nothing in his letters except to assure her that the children were settling in to their school and that all was for the best.

This evening she wondered about them both, Andrew and Jessica – golden Californians now. Were they married? Very probably. Californians married younger, divorced sooner. Was she a grandmother? Very possibly. His name might be Hank or Bud or Junior. Or were those all old names? Why did she think it was a grandson, it might be a girl, a little girl in a sunhat like Jessica had been the day they took her away. She had a Californian clock in her mind always, ever since they left twenty years ago. She never paused and said, "I wonder what time it is out there," she always knew. It was coming up to a quarter to eleven in the morning for them. It was always that when she came round the corner to the Lilac Bus. And she didn't know if they were married or single, working in universities or as domestics. She didn't know if they were happy or wretched, she didn't even know if they were alive or dead.

She slipped neatly in beside Rupert on the back seat, passing young Dee Burke who had been looking so troubled for the last Lord knows when, it was amazing she hadn't cracked up. Past the odd young Nancy Morris. What a cuckoo in the nest that little one was – her mother was a grand little woman altogether, and Deirdre who had gone to the States was very nice, whenever she came back, full of chat. The brother in Cork was a nice lively fellow too. What had come over Nancy to make her so prissy or whatever it was she had become?

Rupert was wearing a new jacket which obviously thrilled him to the core. It just looked like an ordinary teddy boy jacket to Judy, but then she was the first to admit she knew nothing about smart clothes. Dee Burke had gone into ecstasies over it and Rupert had flushed with pleasure.

"It's a birthday present," he whispered as the bus started. "I'll tell you all about it later."

She didn't want to hear all about it on the bus, not while her hip was aching and her head was throbbing, and that young Morris girl might well pretend not to be listening but was only two feet away from them. She felt old tonight. She was years older than everyone on the bus except Mikey Burns and she was a good few years beyond him too. She was twenty years older than the young couple who had set up the health shop and who would be dismantling it within six weeks unless there was a miracle and they discovered the Elixir of Youth and bottled it in expensive but appealing packaging. Surely she was past all this rattling backwards and forwards across the country. Surely she should have some peace and settle down, in one place or the other.

She rooted in her big bag and gave Rupert a small parcel. "It's Green Tea," she said, "Just a little to see if you like it."

His eyes lit up. "This is what you make the mint tea, the proper mint tea with?" he said.

"Yes, a handful of fresh mint, a little sugar in a glass, and you make the tea separately in a silver pot if you have one and then pour it on the mint leaves."

Rupert was very pleased. "I'd been making it with tea bags since we came back from Morocco, and it tasted really terrible, but out there it was like heaven. Oh I AM grateful to you Judy."

"It's only a little," she said warningly.

"Look on it as a sample. If we like it we'll come in and buy kilos of the stuff and make your shop do a roaring trade."

"It would need it." She told him about the kind of trade they were doing. He was reassuring, it was the same everywhere.

89

He worked in an estate agency. Things were very slow. Houses that would have leaped off the books weren't moving at all. And there were shops closing down all over the place. But these things went in phases, he said. Things had to get better soon, the kind of people who knew about these things were confident, that's what you had to remember. Judy said wryly that the kind of people who knew about such things could probably still afford to be confident, they had so many irons in the fire. It was the rest of the world that was the problem.

They felt like old friends the way they talked. She asked him to come and advise for a bit at the cutting of the elderflower, and to help choose some of the dried rosemary and lemon balm for the little herb pillows she was making. Rupert said that for the Christmas trade she should make dozens of those and sell them herself to big shops in Grafton street – they would make great Christmas gifts. Fine, Judy said, but what about her own shop, the shop she worked in? That's the one she wanted to help, not big stores which would make money anyway.

He told her about a politician's wife who had come into the auctioneer's and enquired politely about the location of her husband's new flat. Somehow they all knew that this flat was not a joint undertaking and that the wife was trying to find out. Everyone in the place had copped on and they all became vaguer and more unhelpful by the minute. Eventually the woman had stormed out in a rage. And they had drafted an immensely tactful letter to the politician pointing out that his nest had not been revealed but was in danger of coming under siege.

"Poor stupid woman," said Judy. "She should have let him install a harem in there if it kept him happy."

"You wouldn't have let him do that, you'd have too much spirit," Rupert said admiringly.

"I don't know. I let a man walk away with my two babies twenty years ago. That wasn't showing much spirit, was it?" Judy said.

Rupert gasped. Never had Judy Hickey mentioned the amazing happening that the whole town knew about in garbled versions. He had asked his mother who had said that nobody knew the whole ins and outs of it, and that Rupert's father who had been the local solicitor then also, had been very annoyed because nobody consulted him, and he was the obvious person to have been brought in on it. But there had been something about a Garda charge and a lot of conversation and a solicitor from Dublin coming down for Jack Hickey and then documents being drawn up and Jack and the two children going to America and never coming back.

"But people must know WHY," Rupert had insisted.

His mother said there were more explanations than there were days in the year.

She had been only six years married and twenty now without her man and her children, but she always kept the name Hickey. It was in case the children ever came back, people said. There was a while when she used to go into the town seventeen miles away and ask at the tourist office if you could get the lists of American tourists or just those with children. There was a while she would go up to the bus tours that sometimes came through Rathdoon and scan the seats for nine year old boys with seven year old sisters. But all that was long in the past. If it was so long in the past, why had she mentioned them now?

"Are they on your mind then?" Rupert asked gently. She replied as naturally as if she was in the habit of talking about them. She spoke with no more intensity than she had talked of the mint tea.

"They are and they aren't. We'd probably have nothing to say to each other at this stage."

"What kind of work does he do now? He's not retired, is he?"

"Who? Andrew, he's only your age. I HOPE he hasn't retired yet." She looked amused.

"No, I meant your husband. I didn't know whether your

children were boys or girls." Rupert felt he had put his foot in it.

"Boy and girl, Andrew and Jessica. Andrew and Jessica."

"Nice names," he said foolishly.

"Yes, they are nice names aren't they? We spent ages choosing them. No, I've absolutely no idea whether Jack Hickey is working or whether he is lying in a gutter being moved on by big American cops with sticks. And I don't know if he ever worked in California or whether he lived off his brother. I never cared. Honestly I never gave him a thought. It sounds like someone protesting, I know it does, but it's funny: I have great trouble remembering what he looked like then and I never until this moment wondered how he's aged. Possibly got fatter. His elder brother Charlie was a lovely man, he was fat, and there was a family picture I remember, and the parents were fat."

Rupert was silent for a moment. Such obvious indifference was chilling. You could understand hate or bitterness even. You could forgive a slow fire of rage and resentment. But she talked about him just as you would about some minor celebrity who had been in the news one time. Is he dead or alive? Who knows, who remembers? On to another topic.

"And do the children, well . . . do Andrew and Jessica keep in touch even a little bit?"

"No. That was the agreement."

If he was ever to know, it would be now. He inclined his head slightly to see if anyone else was listening. But no, Dee was fast asleep with her head at an awkward angle, and that awful Morris girl was asleep too. The others were too far ahead to hear.

"That was a harsh sort of agreement," he said tentatively.

"Oh they thought they were justified. People used to think it was quite justifiable to hang a sheep stealer, don't forget."

"Is that what you did?" he asked smiling, "Steal a

92

sheep?"

"Would that it had been so simple. No no, I thought you knew, I thought your father might have told you. No, I was a dope peddler. That's even worse than anything, isn't it?"

She looked like a mischievous girl the way she said it. He felt she couldn't be serious.

"No, what was it about really?" he laughed.

"I told you. I was the local drugs person." She spoke without pride or shame. Just as if she was saying what her name was before she was married. Rupert had never been so startled. "You do surprise me," he said hoping he was managing to keep the shock out of his voice. "But that was YEARS ago."

"It was the sixties. I suppose it is years ago, but your lot aren't the first to know about drugs, you know – the sixties had their own scene."

"But wasn't that only in America and England? Not like now."

"Of course it was here too, not in huge housing estates, and not kids and not heroin. But with brightish, youngish things, at dances, and people who just left College who had been abroad, and it was all very silly, and to this day I think perfectly harmless."

"Hash, was it?"

"Oh yes, Marijuana, pot, a few amphetamines, a bit of LSD."

"You had acid? YOU had acid?" He was half-admiring, half-shocked.

"Rupert, what I had was everything that was going, that wasn't the point. The point was that I was supplying it, and I got caught."

"Why on earth were you doing that?"

"Out of boredom in a way, I suppose. And the money was nice, not huge but nice. And there was a lot of fun too, you met great people – not dead-wood people like Jack Hickey. I was very stupid really. I deserved all that happened. I often think that." She had paused to muse.

Rupert mused with her for a bit. Then he spoke again:

"Were you doing it for long? Before you were caught?"

"About eighteen months. I was at a party and we all smoked something, Lord knows what it was called – I thought it was great, Jack had said nothing at the time, but when we got home he roared and shouted, and said that if this ever happened again, and what he'd do and what he wouldn't do."

"Had he refused it then?"

"Ah you didn't know our Jack, not at all, he had passed the poor little cigarette with the best but he had kept his mouth closed and only pretended to inhale. He was sober and furious. Oh, there was a barney that went on all week, then the ultimatum: if I ever touched it again . . . curtains, he'd take the children off to America, I'd never see them again, no court in the land . . . you could write it out yourself as a script and it would be right, it would be what he said." Rupert listened, fascinated. Judy's soft voice went on:

"Well, Jack was dealing with the livestock. It wasn't like a farm, you know, the house then, it was like a ranch: there were only livestock – no milking, no hens, no crops, just beasts in the field – buy them, graze them, sell them. We had poor old Nanny, she had been my Nanny in the days of old decency and she minded Andrew and Jessica, I used to go here and there. Gathering material for a book on the wild flowers of the West. Gathering bad company more likely. Anyway, because I had my little car and because I went here and there what could be more natural than I go to Dublin or to London as I did twice to get some stuff for people. Others suggested it, I took it up like a flash."

"It's like a story out of a book," Rupert breathed admiringly.

"A horror story then. I remember it as if it was yesterday: acting on information received, warrant, deeply embarassed Mr Hickey, a person of such importance as yourself, absolutely sure there's nothing in it, but have to apply the same laws to the high as to the low, and if we could get it all over as quickly as possible wouldn't that be for the best? Dear, dear, heavens above, what have we here, in MRS Hickey's car, and MRS Hickey's briefcase in the bedroom. And hidden away behind MRS Hickey's books. Well, he was at a loss for words and perhaps Mr Hickey could come up with some explanation?"

She was like an actress, Rupert thought suddenly. He could see the Sergeant or the Superintendent or whoever it was. She could do a one-woman show, the way she was telling the story, and it was without gesture or emphasis since it was being told in a low voice not to wake the others as the minibus sped through the evening.

"It took for ever. And there were people down from Dublin and there was a TD, someone I didn't even know Jack knew. And Jack said that the whole place was becoming too much for him anyway and he had been thinking about selling it for a while, but if there was this scandal then people would know he was doing it under a cloud and the price of the place would drop right down. They were all businessmen, even the guards, they could understand that.

"Then the documents. Jack was going to take the children to his brother unless I signed a sworn statement that I agreed I was an unfit person to act as their mother any longer. The Sergeant could charge me, as soon as Jack had the place sold, his plans made and was off to California with the babies. He begged me to think of the children."

"He did that and yet took them away from you?" Rupert was confused.

"Yes, you see his point was that I was a drugs criminal, that wasn't a good start for any child: they'd be better without me. A deal had been done, kind wise people had seen extenuating circumstances, it was up to me to make the most of them."

She looked out the window for a while.

"I didn't think it would be for ever. I was frightened, I was sure it would all die down. I said yes. He sold the place, well he sold it to that gangster, remember, who conned everyone and went off with a packet. Then the Liquidator or whatever sold it to the nuns and they made it into the conference centre. So now you know the story of the Big House and all the bad people who lived there until the present day." He hadn't realised that she was once mistress of the big Doon House where she now lived in the gate lodge. Today the house had priests, nuns and laypeople coming to do retreats, have discussions. And sometimes there were ordinary conferences that weren't religious at all: that's how the community made the costs of the place. But it was usually a very quiet type of conference where the delegates weren't expecting much of a night life. Rathdoon could offer Ryan's Pub and Billy Burns' chicken and chips; people usually expected more if they came a long way to a conference.

"I had to leave Doon House within a month. But he tricked me in one way. Even with the slightest hint of a drugs offence in those days you couldn't get into the States. They wouldn't give me a visa. And in order to make the distance as great as possible between poor Andrew and Jessica over there and their mad mother over here Jack arranged that I be charged with a minor offence: possession. It was a nothing, even here, and compared to what I could have been charged with, which was dealing, it was ludicrously light. But then the deal had been done, don't forget. And even being charged with possession kept me out of the States." ·

There was another silence.

"Wasn't that a bad trick to play on you?" Rupert said.

"Yes. Yes. I suppose he thought like the people who burned people in the Inquisition . . . that they were doing the right thing. You know, rooting out evil."

"It was very drastic, even for the sixties wasn't it?"

"Will you stop saying the sixties as if it was the stone age. YOU were born in the sixties, don't forget."

"I don't remember much about them," Rupert grinned.

"No. Well I suppose you'd call it drastic; Jack would have called it effective. He was a great man for getting the job done." She spoke with scorn: "That's all he cared about. That's done, he'd say proudly. It was the same coping with me. But Rupert, did you not know all this before? I mean, I don't want to make out that the whole town talks of me morning, noon and night, but I would have thought that you must have heard some drift of it?"

"No, never. I knew that the children had gone away with their father and I think I asked why but I was never told."

"That's because you're so nicely brought up! They're too well bred in your house, they'd never talk of other people's business."

"I think my mother'd be glad to if she knew about it. And it's not only us. I once asked Celia why you didn't have your children, and she said there was some desperate row years ago when judges were even worse than they are today. That's all, nobody knows about the . . . er . . . the smoke and things."

"I don't know whether to be pleased or disappointed," Judy laughed. "I always thought people believed I was up to no good with all the herbal remedies, bordering on the witch doctor nearly."

"I'm afraid people think that's very worthy, we'll have to make your image more villainous for you," Rupert said.

"Oh for ages the unfortunate guards used to come and inspect my herb garden. I had a map of it for them in the end, and told them they must come in whenever they liked and that I would explain anything that looked a bit amiss. Then by the time I went to Dublin, they'd more or less written me off as a dangerous drugs pusher."

"You mean you're in the clear at last, after twenty years?"

"I don't know: sometimes I see the imprint of heavy boots round the camomile beds. Eternal vigilance."

"Do you hate Jack Hickey for it?"

"No, I said to you I never think of him. But you'd

probably find that hard to believe, especially when I think of the children a lot, and to all intents and purposes I don't know them at all. They're strangers to me."

"Yes," Rupert obviously did find it hard to understand.

"It's the same with your mother, you know. Even though she doesn't let on, she thinks of you every day up in Dublin, she is aware of you in a way that it's hard to explain."

"Oh, I don't think so."

"I know it, I asked her once, just to know whether I was odd. She said that when you were away at school it was the same and at university and then when you went into the company. She says that often in her day she pauses and wonders what Rupert's doing now."

"Heavens," he said.

"Not for long, just for a second, you know, not brooding. But I expect you don't pause and wonder what she's doing."

"No, well I think of them a lot, of course, and since Father's been so badly and everything. I DO think of them of course," he said somewhat defensively.

"Stop getting upset, I was only using you as an example. Even if Andrew and Jessica had lived with me until they were grown-up they might still be away and not thinking about me any more. It's the way things happen."

"You're dead easy to talk to, I wish I could talk to my mother like I talk to you. She's much older of course," he added tactfully.

"She is indeed, she could nearly be *my* mother too, but that's not the point . . . You can never talk to your own mother, it's a law of nature."

She smiled and looked out the window, and when that Nancy Morris started talking sense for once about how to relax neck muscles she joined in. She was afraid that young Rupert Green had too much of the Meaning Of Life and the Wronged Woman's viewpoint. She decided to let him snuggle back into his expensive Italian jacket and dream whatever his dreams were.

She always got on better with young people. Someone once said she should have been a teacher but she said no, that would have been putting herself on the other side of the desk from them. But she had much more young friends than people her own age. Bart Kennedy, for example. She could talk to Bart till the cows came home, and she only exchanged the time of day with his father. Kev Kennedy up there in the front of the bus, he was another story: it was very hard going having a chat with Kev. He'd remind you of a young lad who'd been posted at a doorway to give a warning when the master was approaching. And she liked Celia and Dee, she thought, looking round the bus. And young Tom Fitzgerald, he was a great lad. You couldn't like Nancy Morris but she wasn't young anyway. Despite her years she was an old woman and always had been.

And the young people of Rathdoon had always been a great help to her with the things she grew in the small bit of land that Jack Hickey had given her twenty long years ago. She was DIFFERENT to other people, they told her: she didn't pass judgement on them all, she didn't tell them they should be married, or settled down, or more provident or less drinky. And even though they may have thought she was half cracked they came and helped her dig and pick and dry and pack.

She never found the house lonely, no more than the flat in Dublin. Not after all this time. She liked her own company, she ate meals at odd times, she would listen to music at midnight if she liked. In the flat she wore padded earphones and thought she must look like some ageing raver if anyone could see her, but it was a house with many bedsits and flats and you couldn't wake civil servants and people who worked in big office blocks by playing your music through their walls. She did not feel the need of headphones in the lonely little lodge that was all Jack Hickey gave her from the big house. There was nobody near enough to hear, and the birds seemed to like hearing concertos and symphonies. They came and sat on the fence

99

to listen more carefully.

The first time Tom had dropped her there he said he'd wait till she turned on the light. She had been pleased. He had enough nature in him to make sure that she got in safely. But then he was like all the youngsters she knew nowadays, far more natural and a lot more decency in them than the bombasts of her time. Like young Chris and Karen who ran the health shop. They cared so much about it, they never wanted to be rich, to find a good line in anything which would be a snazzy seller and move quickly. They knew none of the jargon of the middle aged businessman, and because they *were* idealistic and simple about things they were going to go to the wall. Her heart was heavy thinking about them. Maybe over in California somewhere Jessica and her husband, if she had one, were starting a health shop. Suppose they were in difficulties, wouldn't it be great if some kind older person were to help?

Judy only had a life interest in her gate lodge, she couldn't sell it even if she wanted to. She only rented her bedsitter in Dublin, she had no savings. Once she had saved the fare to America and kept the post office book thumbed and touched so often it was almost illegible. She had it always in her handbag and would finger it as if it were the ticket to the States. But not now. And she would love so dearly to be able to contribute to Chris and Karen and their dream. Because it was her dream, that shop too. They could make her a director or some such nonsense. If only she had a small lump sum and a regular little subsidy for them instead of taking a small wage from their very sparse little till.

She told Rupert not to waste his weekend coming up to help her in the garden. He had come home to be with his parents and he might as well stay in Dublin if he didn't spend his time with his dying father and give his mother some lift by being in the house all weekend. She was very firm about this, even when he said he'd like the work and the exercise. There'd be plenty of time for all that later. Let him not waste the last months or weeks of his father's life digging and hoeing in a stranger's garden.

"You're not a stranger, Judy, you're a friend,' Rupert had said. She had been pleased at that too.

It was a bright sunny September Saturday. The place seemed to be full of activity. You got weekends when that happened, when Rathdoon seemed to hum with excitement and you got other weekends when not even a tornado coming down Patrick Street would shake them up. She saw Nancy Morris prowling up and down as if she was looking for lost treasure, Kev Kennedy was in and out of his father's shop with a face on him that made it clear the Mafia had put out a contract on him that morning. Every time you stepped out on the road there was someone driving into town that would nearly mow you down. Mrs Casey's ramshackle car with Nancy Morris's mother in it, Mikey Burns going round the place with a set face on him, either doing messages or taking his brother Billy's children blackberrying. He was preoccupied to a degree she had never known. She saw Celia too during the day driving a car with the intent look of someone in a rally. Her mother was beside her and the back of the car was filled with some kind of luggage under a rug. Tom FitzGerald came in for a couple of hours to help in the garden, saying that since he hadn't had one single cross word from any member of his family or their spouses he felt things were too good to be true and he wouldn't risk staying in their company one more minute in case the whole thing would fall apart. She saw Dee Burke driving her mother to town, her face empty and sad, her mother talking away without seeing any emptiness at all beside her. Imagine anyone thinking the country was quiet. Some weekend she must ask Karen and Chris to come and stay – some bank holiday, if they were still in business.

Red Kennedy come in to help his brother Bart.

"Would these make a lot in Dublin?" he asked, looking at the little boxes of seeds.

Judy reflected: "Not a lot, in a way, we're just the wrong size. If it were a one-woman operation selling them at the side of the road, yes there's a living; otherwise it should really be huge nurseries and big chain stores and all that. Still we struggle on."

But it underlined to her the fruitlessness of it all, and the waste of effort not just from her but from decent young fellows like Bart and Red, like Mikey last week and Tom Fitzgerald's nephews when they were home from school. Was it really fair asking them to help in such a doomed business venture. They never did it for money, there wasn't any, but even in terms of their enthusiasm was it wrong to take so much of that as well? She thought of Chris and Karen in Dublin, anxious and also anxious on HER behalf. They felt they owed her a place and a living because she had been so solidly supportive for them. How she wished that there had been a letter from a firm of American solicitors saying that the late James Jonathan Hickey of San Francisco, California had left her a legacy and that her two children were going to fly over and deliver it personally. She often had fantasies about the children arriving, but this was the first time she had thought about the money. Yes, she'd even take a legacy from Jack even if the children didn't deliver it. Anything to help Chris and Karen.

Soon she called a halt to the work. Judy's great success was that she stopped her helpers before they got tired.

There were huge glasses of her elderflower wine which some said was better and reached you more powerfully than anything that was pulled as a pint down in Ryan's. They sat on a wall in the sun and drank it, and the Kennedys went home.

It was dark in the small house and she felt well when she had washed the earth off. She lay out on her window seat with her hands behind her head.

"You look like a cat," Rupert said as he came in. The

door was never closed in summer, never locked in winter.

"That's good. Cats are very relaxed," Judy said.

"Are you relaxed?" he wanted to know.

"Not in my head. My head is worrying about inessential things like money. I never worried about money before."

"I suppose it was always easy to get it before."

"Yes, well in the old days I told you how I got it, but since then I haven't needed it much. Now, I'd like to keep the shop open, that's all."

Rupert sat down on a rocking chair that squeaked. He got up immediately and went for the oil.

She thanked him, but said his mother had a rocking chair, he should be sitting on that.

"There's nothing to say, I had to escape for a little bit," he pleaded.

"Only a little," Judy said.

"It's just that he tried to talk. He asks are there many houses on the market and things." Rupert had a face full of pain.

"But isn't that good? He's well enough, alert enough to know. Kind enough to care."

"And mother says, that he really likes having me home. But it's nothing. Nothing at all."

"Only if you make it nothing for them." Judy lost her sympathy. She stood up and stretched.

"Listen to me Rupert Green, not one more minute of your father's time am I taking. I'm going for a walk in Jack Hickey's woods." He looked hurt.

"Please boy, please. Think of all those years when you'll say if only I could have just sat there and talked about any old thing. And for your mother, please. I'll meet you and you can buy me a pint of that synthetic stuff they call chilled wine down in Ryan's." He brightened up.

"Will you? That would be nice."

"When he's asleep, when he's had some return from you."

"I'm not THAT bad."

"No, but he was nearly fifty years of age when you arrived in his life and he had to be woken up with your teething and your screaming and then you didn't come into his office: he couldn't put Green and Son. It's Green and MacMahon. Go on, sit with him, talk about anything. It doesn't matter if it seems formal and meaningless, you're there, you're trying . . . that's all that matters."

"And what time will we go to Ryan's?" He was eager.

"RUPERT! Will you give over, this is not a date. Ryan's is not a cocktail lounge, it's the only bar in Rathdoon, I'll be down there when I feel like it and you come when your father's well asleep and you've had a bit of time with your mother."

"Around nine or so?" he said desperate to be specific.

"Around nine or so," she said resignedly.

She put on her boots. It was a long time since she had walked the woods. The three nuns who ran the ecumenical conferences and the diocesan seminars in the big house knew vaguely that Mrs Hickey in the gate lodge had once lived in the big house. They were always polite to her and encouraged her to wander around if she ever felt like it. They were possibly relieved that the wildish looking woman in the gypsy style headscarves didn't take them up too often on their offer. She never went anywhere near the house but she had told them it was nice to be able to feel free to walk under those old trees and pick flowers. Sometimes she would leave a great bunch of bluebells at their door, wrapped up in damp leaves. She never rang or asked to be entertained in the parlour. It was an ideal relationship.

Today she walked more purposefully. She didn't just stroll following a whim or a line of young saplings. No, today she knew where she was heading.

It was still there in among the ivy covered trees. Wild now, but hidden from the most determined searchers because of that old fallen tree. It looked as if there was nothing beyond. She eased herself over the tree and stood once more in her own little marijuana grove. She saw the cannabis plants that she had begun twenty-two years ago, many dead, many seeded and wasted. Some living though, some needing only a little attention.

It wouldn't take her long to find a proper outlet in Dublin. It must be done well away from the shop, Chris and Karen must never know.

She felt as strongly about this as her husband had felt that Andrew and Jessica must never know.

She felt the old quickening under her heart. It would be exciting to be back in the business again after all these years.

Kev

Kev thought he'd never get away from the Pelican. The Pelican was in one of those good moods, very rarely seen of late, where he'd ramble on about people known only to himself. There was a cast of thousands in the Pelican's stories and the same people never appeared twice. Kev listened attentively because if you missed the bit where your man came in one day and your other man was already in there and your old fellow came out the other door then you lost the whole grasp of it, and the Pelican might easily snap some kind of a question at you to make sure you were on the ball.

Kev was only afraid of the Pelican; he was *terrified* of some of the others. But even though the Pelican was not the highest in the terror stakes Kev would have let the Lilac Bus go to Rathdoon without him rather than risk insulting this man whose big hooked nose was the cause of his name. You didn't mess with the Pelican, Kev didn't know much, but he knew that much.

Fortunately the Pelican was hailed by someone more interesting and Kev was released; he sprinted round the corner. The bus was almost full. But he wasn't the last. Mikey Burns was rubbing his hands: oh please may he not have any quiz games tonight. Mikey was perfectly nice when he quietened down, but all this "I say I say I say" like one of those comics on a music hall show on telly. And he was no GOOD at it, that was what was so hopeless, he always laughed in the wrong place. It would have been nice to sit beside Celia; that's what he liked best: she'd address about five civil sentences to him and then she'd leave him to his own thoughts, as she looked out the window. Or Rupert, he was a quiet fellow too, and not toffee-nosed or anything. Kev's brothers Bart and Red were always surprised that he didn't seem to know Mrs Hickey better. They were mad about her: in fact his Da was always saying that they'd go over to her place and dig her witch's brews in the garden and her lavender and her forget-me-nots and they wouldn't dig their own potatoes like men. Mrs Hickey was nice enough, but she had a disconcerting way of looking right through you when she was talking, as if she didn't want any small talk. Neither did Kev of course want any small talk, but he didn't want that dark intense face with those X-ray eyes looking at him either. He always got the feeling that she saw just a little bit too much.

Kev worked in Security, well not real security with helmets and coshes and alsatians and vans with no hand signals. More like being a porter really or a commissionaire but it was called security. When anyone phoned down to the front desk to ask if a letter had been delivered by hand or if a visitor had arrived Kev answered the phone with the words, "Hallo. Security?"

Once he had got a phone call from his father asking him to bring down boxes of some new potato crisp that had been advertised on the television and the place was going mad looking for it. Kev's father had been so entertained by Kev calling himself Security that he had threatened to telephone every day just for the sheer pleasure of it. Kev had told him anxiously that they had been told to keep personal calls down to the minimum. But he shouldn't have worried, his father wasn't going to waste good money on hearing the same joke over and over.

Bart and Red didn't know what he came home for every weekend. It wasn't that they didn't want to see him, they were just as happy that he was back as not. But why *every* weekend? That was what would fox you. And he didn't even go to the dance on a Saturday night. And he didn't have a crowd to drink with in Ryan's; he'd go in and out for a couple but he wouldn't have a session there. The Kennedys had little or no conversation with their Da who had a cigarette in his mouth and the radio on full blast from morning to night. It was unlikely to be for company.

Kev knew that he was a bit of a mystery to them. And to Tom Fitzgerald who had explained that the bus only made a profit if he could be sure of his seven passengers on a Friday. That's why he could do it so cheaply. You agreed to come on the bus every Friday for ten weeks, or if you couldn't you'd send someone in your place – not to Rathdoon of course, but part of the way or as far as the big town seventeen miles from home. Or if you could find nobody you still paid for your seat. That way it was half the cost of any other bus going that route and what's more it brought you to the door. Kev was getting out of the bus before ten o'clock and saying goodnight to Nancy Morris who only lived across the street. He was home in Rathdoon safe. He would take a big breath of air and let it all out in a long sigh of relief. Tom often looked at him puzzled, and his father would nod welcomingly over the radio and tell him it was just coming up to the news. A mug of tea might be handed to him and a slice of shop cake cut. They had never known any other kind of cake, Kev and his brothers. Their mother had died long ago and even Bart, who could remember her, never knew her when she was well enough to make bread or cakes. When the news was over his father might ask had it been a hard week and were there any savages with crowbars in. He said there were more cases of violence in Dublin than there were in Chicago and he would never set his foot in the city again without an armed guard. Kev had tried to argue with him in the beginning, but now he didn't bother. Anyway, nowadays he was beginning to think his father was right.

Nobody at work knew where Kev went at weekends: they all thought that he was some kind of lay monk or something and that he went to do good works but part of the goodness was that you didn't talk about it. The kind old Mr Daly, one of the nicest people Kev had ever met, would shake his head in its uniform cap full of admiration.

"I don't know why they give out about the younger generation," old Mr Daly would say, "I really don't. There's that young Kev who works with us in the front hall, and he's off giving soup to winos and praying in front of the Blessed Sacrament, and teaching illiterates to read. Gone out of here like a bow from an arrow at six o'clock and we never hear hair nor hide of him until Monday morning."

Kev had never told one word of this fabrication to Mr Daly or to anyone else. But having heard it, and seen that it was accepted he let it pass. After all if anyone came nosing around and asking questions, wasn't it better that old Mr Daly and John and the others thought he was with the Simon Community or the Legion of Mary rather than knowing he caught a lilac-coloured minibus as regularly as clockwork and sped out of Dublin and all its danger every Friday night.

Just suppose for one sickening minute that Daff or Crutch Casey or the Pelican came round upset over something, well there was nothing they could be told. Nobody knew where Kev went at weekends.

He had always had this secrecy, even when he was a young fellow. He remembered Bart telling a total stranger in the shop that their mother was dead, that she had died in the hospital after two months and a week. Kev would never have given that information to a woman who had come in to buy bars of chocolate and ice cream for the children in the car. No matter how nice she had been, no matter how much she had praised the three young lads serving in the shop because their father was out getting the shed at the back built to hold the gas cylinders and the briquettes. Kev would have told her nothing and put his arm in his mouth which was a great way to stop having a conversation. But Bart and Red would tell anyone anything . . . Bart even told about the time when Kev was seventeen and he had tried to get Deirdre Morris, who was the much nicer sister of Nancy, to come into a field with him and swore it was to show her a nest of small birds.

Deirdre Morris had thrown back her head laughing, pushed him over so that he fell in the mud and had gone home laughing. "A nest of small birds – is that what they call it nowadays?" Kev was shocked. To admit to such a lustful thing and even worse to admit to such a defeat. But no, Bart thought it was a scream, and that time that Deirdre had come back from America married with a baby called Shane, Bart was still able to laugh over it with her. And Red was the same, a demon dancer and he'd tell half the country their business, and about how they should have got an agency for tarmacadamming the place but his Da hadn't moved quick enough and Billy Burns had got it first. Kev told nothing. But then Kev had much more to hide.

Celia arrived just after him and the doors were closed. They were off. Round the corner and through the open door of the pub he could the Pelican holding a pint in one hand and a rolled up newspaper in the other. A rolled paper was a great thing for making a point, for emphasising something, And that was the Pelican's style. Emphasising things.

Mikey was unfortunately in top form tonight: tricks with matches and a glass, have them rolling in the aisles in a pub. Didn't poor Mikey realise that it was only drunks that suddenly started doing match tricks in a pub, or lonely people, or madmen. Not ordinary people unless they were all in a group of friends, and if you had a group of friends why would you need to do tricks anyway? He was explaining how to weight the matchbox; Kev looked out the window and saw the housing estates outside Dublin flashing by. Old Mr Daly said to him that any day now Kev would find himself a young woman and they'd save for a house in a place like that and there'd be no knowing him ever after. People like Mr Daly and Mikey knew nothing about the real world. There was Mikey going on about how you weighted the matchbox deliberately with a twopenny piece in it and it always fell over on the side you'd put the coin in, so you could bet someone that it would always fall on the side you said. Kev had looked at him vacantly.

"I bet you Bart or Red Eddie would love a trick like that," Mikey muttered. Kev knew they would. They had the time and the peace of mind to enjoy it.

Kev never told Mikey that he was a porter too in a way. Well security really, but it was the same field. He never told any of them where he worked, except that it was in the big new block. You could be doing anything there, literally anything. They had civil servants and they had travel agencies, and airlines and small companies with only two people in them, they had a board in the hall with a list a mile long of the organisations who were tenants of the building. Kev just said he worked there; when anyone asked him what he did, he said this and that. It was safer. One morning he was standing there in his uniform and he saw Dee Burke coming. She was going with some papers to a solicitor on the fifth floor. Mr Daly phoned up and announced her and Kev had sorted furiously on the floor for something so she didn't see him. Later he wondered why. It couldn't matter whether Dee Burke knew that he worked at the front desk of the big new office block. She hardly thought when she went to buy her cigarettes at the Kennedy shop that their youngest son was the chairman of some company up in Dublin. He didn't even want her to think he was in a clerical job. Why hide then? Wiser. Like not walking on cracks in the road. No reason but it just *seemed* the right thing to do.

Of course in a way it was all this secrecy that had him where he was. If he had been a different type he'd never have got into this mess at all.

It began on his birthday, he was twenty-one. It was an

114

ordinary working day. His father had sent him a ten pound note in a card with a pink cat on it. Bart and Red Eddie had said that there would be great drink in Ryan's next Friday on account of it. Nobody else knew. He hadn't told Mr Daly in case the old man might get a cake and embarrass him; he didn't tell anyone back up in the house where he had a room. They kept to themselves a lot and if they heard him saying he was twenty-one they'd feel they had to do something for him. He didn't tell anyone up at the pigeons either. In the lofts they didn't have time for birthdays and such things. So that day nobody in Dublin knew that Kevin, youngest son of Mr Michael Kennedy, shop proprietor, and the late Mrs Mary Rose Kennedy of Rathdoon had now reached twenty-one. He thought of it a lot all morning and somehow it began to seem over-important to him. Other people had records played for them on radio programmes, other people who were twenty-one had cards, lots of them, not just one. Dee Burke had a party in a hotel – he remembered hearing about it just a couple of months back; Bart and Red had been invited and Bart said he couldn't get into a monkey suit but Red the demon dancer had hired one and had a great time. And even his own brothers had bits of celebration. Bart and all his pals had a barbecue down by the river; those were before every Tom, Dick and Harry were having barbecues. They roasted a bit of beef and ate it between doorsteps of bread and it was gorgeous, and there'd been great singing and goings on. And when Red was twenty-one two years back there had been a crowd of them who had all come to the house for a few drinks and a cake then they'd got into a truck and driven off to the dance. But nothing at all for Kev.

It got in on his mind. He made an excuse to Mr Daly and said that he wanted to go out the back for a half an hour. He didn't feel well. Mr Daly was so concerned that he immediately felt ashamed. Those were the days before he had been a regular disappearer at weekends, before Mr Daly had assumed that he was an unsung and uncanonised saint.

He sat out in the loading area as it was called, a place where vans could come with deliveries of paper, or messengers on those big motor bikes with speaking handlebars could leave their machines. He took out a cigarette and thought about other fellows his age and wondered why he had been so anxious to get away and why he had ever thought it would be any better. Four men were loading a van efficiently. A fifth was standing leaning on a crutch and staring around him idly. Into the van were going sanitary fittings, handbasins, lavatories, small water heaters. Without haste but with commendable speed they loaded.

Kev dragged his cigarette. They must be getting new fitments somewhere upstairs, that looked like a big contract. Wait. He hadn't seen any of them come through security, and everyone had to come to the front desk. Even if they went straight out the door again and were sent round to the loading bay. The rules said desk first.

His eyes took on the merest flicker of interest but it was enough to alert the man with the bent leg leaning so casually on the crutch.

"Not wearing a cap, didn't notice him," he said out of the corner of his mouth.

A big man with a beak-shaped nose paused momentarily and then slid from the human chain which was stacking the fitments. He strolled over to Kevin whose stomach knotted in fright. He realised like a shower of cold rain coming down his gullet that this was a Job, these were five men taking fitments OUT of the new building, fitments that would turn up again in houses all over the city. He swallowed hard.

The Pelican walked slowly: he didn't look a bit furtive, nor did he look worried.

"Can I have a smoke?" he asked casually. Behind him the loading continued regular as clockwork, innocent as anything.

"Yes. Um," Kev handed him the packet.

"What are you doing with yourself here?" The Pelican's

eyes narrowed.

The question was perfectly polite. It could have been a gentle enquiry of any fellow lounger on a summer morning. He might even have added something like "on this fine day". But he hadn't. The Pelican and all of them were waiting to know what Kevin would say and Kevin knew that what he said now was probably going to be the most important question he ever answered in his life.

"It's my twenty-first birthday," he said. "And I got annoyed sitting inside there in Security and nobody knowing, so I thought I'd come out here and have a bit of a smoke anyway to celebrate."

There was absolutely no doubt that what he said was true. You didn't need a lie detector or the experience of years with truth drugs to know that Kev Kennedy had given a perfectly accurate account of why he was there, and something about him made the Pelican believe that there was going to be no trouble here.

"Well, when we're finished here maybe we'll buy a drink at your lunch hour. A fellow shouldn't be twenty-one and have nobody know."

"That's what I think," Kev said eagerly, averting his eyes from the biggest and most barefaced theft from the building where he was meant to be part of Security. It seemed to be winding up now, the convoy were closing the doors and getting into the van.

"So, what is it? One o'clock?" the Pelican's nose was like a scythe so large and menacing did it appear, and his eyes were like two slits.

"It's a bit difficult at lunchtime, you see I only get forty-five minutes and I suppose you'll be moving on out of the area," Kev's face was innocent.

"But where would you like your birthday drink then and when?" There was no area for argument in the proposal, only a small margin of latitude for the time and place.

"Well, wherever you like of course, and at about six. Is that all right?"

Kev was eager. The Pelican nodded. He named a city centre pub.

"We'll give you a drink each, and as you no doubt saw there's five of us, so that's five drinks."

"Oh, God, that would be great altogether," Kev said. "Are there five of you? I didn't notice."

The Pelican nodded approvingly. He swung his way back to the van and in beside the driver who looked like a champion wrestler.

"Six o'clock," he called cheerfully out the window.

It wasn't discovered until four thirty. A lot of offices on the sixth floor weren't occupied yet. Some people just assumed that the bathrooms were being refitted, and sighing had gone to other floors. It was only when one of the secretaries said she was getting dropped arches and told Mr Daly that it was an extraordinary thing to think that brand new cloakrooms should be redone within three months that any kind of alarm was raised. The broad-daylightness of it all staggered them. The guards were called, the confusion was enormous. Kev had difficulty in getting away by six. He was ninety per cent sure that they wouldn't be there. They could be walking into a trap for all they knew. How were they to know that they were dealing with Kev Kennedy who never told anybody anything? They might have assumed he would have plain-clothes guards drinking pints of shandy all round the pub. But just in case. And just in case they came back and dealt with him. After all they knew where he worked, he knew nothing about them.

They were all there.

"There was a bit of commotion at work, I got delayed," he said.

"Ah, you would all right," said the Pelican generously. He was introduced to Daff and John, and Ned and Crutch Casey.

"What's your real name?" he asked the man with the twisted leg.

"Crutch," the man said, surprised to be asked.

They each bought him a pint and they raised their glasses solemnly and said Happy Birthday at each round. By the fourth round he was feeling very wretched. He had never drunk more than three pints in Ryan's and never more than two anywhere else. Ryan's led you to be daring because even if you fell down you got home on all fours without too much difficulty.

Daff was the man like a wrestler. Kev wondered why he was called that but he decided it might not be wise. Daff bought the last drink and handed Kev an envelope.

"We were sorry to see a culchie all on his own with no-one to wish him a happy birthday, so that's a small present from Pelican, Crutch, John, Ned and me." He smiled as if he were a foolish, generous uncle dying for the nephew to open the electric train set and begin to call out with excitement.

Kev politely opened the envelope and saw a bundle of blue twenty pound notes. The room went backwards and forwards and began to move slowly around to the left. He steadied himself on the bar stool.

"I couldn't take this, sure you don't know me at all."

"And you don't know us," Daff beamed.

"Which is as it should be," the Pelican said approvingly.

"But I'd not know you, without ... without this, you know."

He looked at the envelope as if it contained explosives. There were at least six notes, maybe more. He didn't want to count them.

"Ah but this is better, this MARKS the day for all of us, why don't we meet here every week around this time, and if you've that invested properly then you could buy us a drink, and slowly we could sort of GET to know each other."

Kev's mouth felt full of lemon juice.

"Well I'd love to ... sort of keep in touch with you all ... but, honestly, this is too much. Like, I mean, I'd feel bad."

"Not at all, you wouldn't," smiled the Pelican and they

119

were gone.

Every Tuesday since he had met them; sometimes it was just a drink. Sometimes it was more. Once it had been a driving job. He would never forget it to his dying day. They went into a new block of flats and carefully unrolled the brand new stair carpet. They had heard that the fitting men were coming that afternoon so they had anticipated the visit by removing every scrap of it. The timing had been of the essence on that one. The expensive wool carpet had arrived that morning; there was only a four-hour period when it could be removed, and that meant watching the flats very carefully in case any untoward enquiries were made. It was all completely successful, of course, like all their enterprises seemed to be. Kev had taken a day off work for the carpet heist but the carpet heist had taken years off his life. He felt as if he had been put down on the street and the whole crowd coming out of Moran Park had walked over him. He couldn't understand how they remained so untouched. Crutch Casey told of horses that had fallen at the last fence. Ned and John were more dog people, they talked of evil minded and corrupt greyhounds who KNEW how to slow down through some instinct. The Pelican told long tales full of people that nobody knew, and Daff seemed to say nothing much but he was as relaxed as a man coming out after a swim about to light his pipe on the beach on a sunny day.

They never told him he HAD to join in, and they didn't ask him so much that he felt he should run away to America to escape them. Often he didn't have to do anything except what they called "re-sorting". That might mean wrapping a whole load of Waterford Glass which arrived from a hotel before it got time to get out of its boxes, into different kind of containers. Each glass to be held carefully and sorted according to type, wrapped in purple tissue paper in gift boxes of six. He became quite an authority on the various designs, or suites as they were called, and decided that the Colleen Suite was his favourite; and that when he got married he would have two dozen Colleen brandy glasses and use them around the house as ordinary everyday glasses, or in the bathroom for his toothbrush. Then he remembered what he was doing and the fantasy would disappear. He would look around the garage and keep parcelling in the nice anonymous gift boxes. He never knew where they went, and what happened to them. He never asked. Not once. That's why they liked him, that's why they trusted him utterly. From that very first day in the loading area they thought he was one of their own, and it was too late now to tell them that he wasn't. The longer it went on, the more ludicrous it would be trying to get out.

On calmer days Kev asked himself what was so terrible. They never took from individuals, they didn't do people's houses and flats: it was companies who had to replace miles of red wool carpet, boxes of prestigious glassware, rooms full of sanitary fittings. They never did over old women, young couples, they never carried a weapon, not even a cosh. In many ways they weren't bad fellows at all. Of course they never actually went out to work in a normal way, and they did lie to people, with their clipboards and their air of being perfectly legitimate. And people did get into trouble after they'd visited places, like poor old Mr Daly who'd been hauled in by everyone and though it was never said, the thought had been in the air that he might be getting too old for the job. And they stole. They stole things almost every week and by no standards could that be a thing that Kev Kennedy from Rathdoon wanted to be in. Or worse, caught in. It was unthinkable. They still talked about that young fellow who was a cousin of the FitzGeralds and worked in their shop for a bit; he was given three years for doing a post office in Cork. The whole of Rathdoon had buzzed with it for months and Mrs FitzGerald, Tom's mother, had said she hoped everyone realised that he wasn't a first cousin, he was a very far out one, and they had tried to give him a start and look at the thanks they got. Could you imagine what old Da would have to go through? And all Red's hopes of getting

121

some gorgeous wife would go for their tea, and poor Bart was so decent and helpful, wouldn't it be a shame on him for ever?

But how did you get out? He couldn't live in a city that contained the Pelican and Daff and Crutch Casey if they thought he had ratted on them. There was no point trying to pretend that he had left town or anything. They knew everything: it was their business to know things, to know when deliveries were expected, when watchmen went for their coffee, when regular porters were on holidays, when managers were young and nervous, when shops were too busy to notice their furniture being loaded into private vans. They knew where Kev lived and worked; he wouldn't dream of lying to them.

But he got out of weekend work. That's when they did some of their bigger jobs, and he wanted to be well away from it. He told them vaguely that he had to go out of town. He had been going home that very first weekend after they met him and so it had seemed a natural continuation, not a new pattern of behaviour. He didn't say it was Rathdoon, he didn't say it was home, but they knew he wasn't lying when he was saying that he went out of town for weekends, Crutch Casey had said goodnight to him one Sunday night outside the house where he had a room, and Kev knew that it was just a routine inspection. He had been cleared now, even the Pelican whom he had met by accident just on the corner knew that he was leaving Dublin for the weekend – he didn't even bother to check.

But how could he get out of working for them mid-week? Some of the jobs were getting bigger and Kev was getting tenser. Once or twice Daff had asked him not to be so jumpy – that he was like some actor playing a nervous crook in an old black and white B movie. It was fine for Daff who didn't have a nerve in his body. Simply fine for him. Others didn't find it so easy. The very sight of a guard was enough to weaken Kev's legs, even the shadow of anyone fairly big was enough to make him jump. Oddly enough it hadn't made him feel guilty about religion: he went to Mass and at Christmas and Easter to communion; he knew that God knew that there wasn't much Sin involved. No Grievous Bodily Harm or anything. But he had never been much of a one for talking to God individually like you were meant to: he didn't feel like putting the question personally. And there was nobody else really BUT God when all was said and done because everyone else would have a very strong view one way or the other, and mainly the other. Like get out of that gang at a rate of knots, Kev Kennedy, and stop acting the eejit.

Mikey's poor kind face was there a few inches from him, Mikey Burns who'd be the kind of bank porter that would get shot in a raid, certainly not like Kev, the kind of security man who had become best buddies with the gang that had ripped off all the fittings from the place he worked. Mikey Burns sleeping with a little smile dreaming about something, jokes with glasses of water and coins maybe, and there was he, Kev, who had driven get-away vans and done watch duty and helped to reparcel stolen goods. Kev felt alien as he looked out at the darkening countryside. Lonely and guilty as hell.

His father told him after the news that Red had notions about a farmer's daughter and was going to bring her to tea during the weekend no less, and they were all to keep their shoes on, talk nicely and put butter on a plate and the milk in a jug. He said that he thought Bart might as well join the Franciscans and put on sandals and carry a begging bowl for all the good he was ever going to do with his life and his share of the business. When he wasn't digging up Mrs Hickey's foxgloves and hemlocks or whatever it was she grew he was helping Mrs Ryan in the pub to stand on her own two shaky legs and serving the customers from behind the bar and not a penny piece was he getting from either of them. He was surprised that Bart hadn't gone into Fitzgerald's shop and said that if they'd like someone to stand there and serve for a few days a week without wages he'd be happy to do it. Kev didn't know what to say to this. He nibbled a slice of cake and thought about the difference between people. There was Daff who had a nice big open face like Bart, organising the transfer of twenty microwave ovens from one warehouse to another by a deceptively simple scheme which involved Ned who was the most forgettable of them all going up with a sheaf of papers, an air of bewilderment and an instruction that they were apparently to go back to have something checked. And there was Bart Kennedy who had a big open face like Daff digging Judy Hickey's garden for her and helping Celia's mother to stay upright in Ryan's. God, what different worlds he moved in; Kev thought with a shudder at the danger of it all.

"Are you not going down to the pub?" his father asked.

"No, I'm tired after the week, and the long journey, I'll just go up and lie on my bed," he said.

His father shook his head: "I really wish I knew what brings you home, you do so little when you arrive, and you've lost your interest in football entirely. You could have been a good footballer if you'd put your mind to it."

"No, I was never any good. You only say that because you wanted a son a county footballer, I'm no good."

"Well what does bring you back here, what are you running from . . ?" He hadn't finished but the cup was in pieces on the floor and Kev's face was snow white.

"Running, what do you mean?"

"I mean is it the violence up there or the dirt, or those blackguards roaming in tribes or what? Haven't you good wages and you're always very generous giving me the few quid here . . . but a young man of your age, you should be up to all kinds of divilment and diversions, shouldn't you?"

"I don't know, Da, I don't think I was ever much good at anything, football, divilment, anything." He sounded very glum.

"Haven't you got a fine job up in one of the finest buildings in the land, and you earn your own living which is more than those two boyos there – oh they're a great pair I have on my hands. One a sort of Martin de Porres going round the place giving half his cloak to everyone he meets, one a dandy who has the bright red hair nearly combed off his scalp and the mirrors nearly cracked in bits staring into them. You're the best of them, Kev, don't be running yourself down."

Kev Kennedy went up to bed without a word, and he lay there as the sounds of Rathdoon which were not very loud went past his window, a small window over the shop, which looked out on the main street.

Red's girl was coming the very next day it turned out, so they all had to do a spring clean on the back room. There were to be cups instead of mugs, a clean cloth was spread and bread was cut on a tray and then put onto a plate to avoid all the crumbs. They took ham and tomatoes from the shop, a bottle of salad cream and Red hardboiled three eggs.

"This is a feast, she'll marry you immediately," Bart said when he saw Red looking speculatively at some of the frozen cakes in the cold food section.

"Quit laughing and keep looking round the room to see what it would look like to a new eye." Red had it bad this time. Her name was Majella and she was an only child, she was used to much greater style than the three Kennedy brothers and their father could provide even if they had been trying seriously. But none of them except Red was making much of an effort: their father wanted to be in his shop, Bart wanted to get over to Judy Hickey and Kev wanted to go off down by the river where he felt nice and quiet and miles from all that was happening at this very moment to microwave ovens in a warehouse in Dublin.

Majella was arriving at five o'clock: her father would give her a lift, but he wouldn't call in, it was much too early for that yet. They did a deal, the brothers. Bart and Kev agreed to wear proper ties and jackets and have polished shoes. Red agreed to go over to Judy Hickey's and put in two hours because she needed it this weekend particularly and because it would keep him calm. There would be no bad language, eating with fingers and picking of teeth, but in return Red would not embarrass them by giving moon faced sick calf impersonations, not would he ask them to delight Majella with stories of their exotic lives. When the bell rang to say that somebody had come into the shop they would go in order of seniority. Da first, then Bart, then Kev, then Da and so on. Red was not to abandon them to talk to Majella on their own.

She was a lovely big girl with no nonsense in her and by the time they had sat her down she was like part of the family. She said they must be great fellows altogether to have the butter on the place and the milk not in a bottle but in a jug. Whenever she went over to her cousin's place they were all putting their dirty knives into the butter at once, they needed a woman to civilise them. Red began to look like a sick calf when she talked of the civilising influence of a woman and he had to be kicked until he dropped it again. Majella said she was going to do the washing up and they could all dry, and seeing out of the corner of her eye that the dishcloths were not all they might be she called to Red to bring a packet of J-cloths out of the shop.

"Isn't it paradise to be here!" she said with a big smile at them all. "Who could want anything better than a shop right off your own living room?"

They had dried up in no time; the big room looked better somehow than it had done for years. Majella said that maybe she and Red might go for a bit of a tour round Rathdoon now and get out of everyone's way. By half past six she had a blushing delighted Red firmly by the arm and was linking him on her own little lap of honour around the community she had decided to join.

"Oh there's no escape there, that knot will be tied, poor Red." Bart laughed good-naturedly about the fate that could well be happening to his brother.

"Will you stop that nonsense: poor Red, my hat!

Wouldn't a girl have to be half mad or have the courage of a lion to marry any one of the three of you." He sounded very pessimistic indeed.

"Would you say she IS mad?" Kev asked interestedly. "She was a very nice class of a girl I thought."

"Of course she's nice, she's far too good for him: the thing is will she realise it in time?" Bart and Kev exchanged glances. Their father seemed to be torn between the delight of having the lovely laughing Majella around the place and the strictly honest course of action which was to warn the girl that his son was a bad bargain.

"Let her work it out for herself maybe?" Bart suggested and his father looked relieved.

Bart had a lot of sense, Kev realised, suddenly. He wasn't just a do-gooder and a big innocent. But he was the other side of the tracks now, he wasn't in the Underworld like Kev was, there could be no talking to him about the problem.

"Would you fancy an early pint down in Ryan's before the mob gets in there?" Bart said to him. Kev was pleased.

"That'd be the way to do it" he said sagely. Their father had gone back to the shop and was twiddling the dial for the news.

They walked down the road. It was quiet – most people were in at their tea; the sound of the half past six news that their father was listening to back in the shop came from several windows. Down past Billy Burns' chip shop. Billy wasn't there today, Mikey and that bright little Treasa who worked there, no sign of the new girl Eileen, well she had always looked too good to spend her day lifting pieces of cod or wings of chicken out of a deep fryer in Rathdoon. They came to the bridge. Bart leaned over and looked at the river. They used to race sticks under the bridge here when they were kids, and there were always so many arguments about whose stick had won Bart invented a system of tying different coloured threads on to each one. It seemed very long ago.

"What's eating you?" Bart asked.

"I don't know what you mean?"

"I'm not the world's brainiest man but I'm not blind either. Tell me, Kev. Can't you? It can't be any worse when you've told me. It might even be a bit better. Like I'm not going to be saying aren't you an eejit or blame you or anything, but there's something terrible wrong up in Dublin, isn't there?"

"Yes" Kev said.

"Before Red fell so much in love that he can't think of anything else, he and I were going to go up there one day on the excursion and try and sort it out, whatever it was."

Kev gulped with gratitude at the thought of his two brothers taking on a heavy gang like Daff, the Pelican, Crutch Casey and their team.

"What did YOU think the problems might be?" he asked nervously, fishing to see had Bart any notion of how bad things were or was he still in a world like the playground of the infants' school.

"I thought it might be a girl you got into trouble, but it's going on too long for that. I thought it might be a debt – you know, poker or the horses – but you don't seem to have any interest in either."

Bart's big innocent face looked puzzled. Kev drew a long breath. Well it seemed that Bart could take on that much anyway. What about the next step, could Bart listen to the story that had begun on his twenty-first birthday a year and a half ago, or would he run for the guards. Kev didn't know. Bart was shaping a stick and tying a bit of string round it.

"Here," he said to Kev, "Let this be yours: I'll beat you any day with my one." They threw the sticks over the side and rushed across to see them coming through. Kev's stick was in front.

"Would you beat that?" Bart seemed surprised. "I've been up here practising and I thought I had the shape of stick that ran best with the flow."

Kev began to tell him, in fact once started it tumbled out of him: a mixture of names and commodities, Crutch Caseys and Microwaves, Daffs and cut glass, Pelicans and Axminster carpet. Kev had no starring role the way he told it, his only stroke of genius had been to go home every weekend on the Lilac Bus to avoid even more major crime in the city at weekends. He was in now and there was no getting out. Bart must know that, they'd all seen the films, they knew the plot. If Kev said to Daff that he'd had enough, thank you, he couldn't answer for the consequences but he knew it'd be awful. He didn't think they'd beat him up: they never used violence, he said almost pleadingly to Bart. But they would punish him. They'd send the guards round to his house or to work, or they'd send a note to Mr Daly accusing Kev of giving the tip-off about the cloakroom fittings that time. It was a nightmare: he was in it for ever.

He hardly dared to look at Bart during some of the confession, and once or twice he gave the odd glance and got the feeling that Bart was half smiling. Maybe he didn't understand the hugeness of it all. Once he was almost certain he got a smile and Bart had hastily put his hand over his face.

"So now, you see I'm caught entirely," he ended.

"I don't think so," Bart said slowly.

"But it's not LIKE here, Bart; you don't know, they're diferent to us. They're not our type of people."

"But they must have thought you were their kind of person otherwise they wouldn't have pulled you in," Bart said.

"But I TOLD you how that happened. I'm not a thief by nature, I'm fairly happy to work for my wages. Not very, but fairly. I'm not any good as a criminal."

"No I don't mean their type as a thief, you're secretive like they are. That's what they liked about you – you're not a blabber about who you know, what you do: that'll make them think you won't blab about them."

"Well I don't – haven't until now, that is."

"So that's how you get out if you want to. Tell them you're in with another lot now. No hard feelings, handshakes, pints all round, and that's it."

"Bart, you haven't any idea . . . ."

"But you see, you keep up this hard man image with them except once or twice when you've had a fit of the shivers. You never try to talk them out of it, or discuss what they do with the stuff. They probably think you're a silent pro and someone has made you a better offer."

"They wouldn't have such a high regard for me as that."

"They must have a very high regard for you if they let you in on all their jobs. No, leave them as you joined them, with no chat, no explanations except the one they are owed. That you've got a new scene."

Bart talking about scenes, Bart saying that these gangsters are owed an explanation – it was like the end of the world.

"I don't think I'd be able to go through with it."

"You were able to join them, that was harder."

"And should I give them back the money?"

"Give them WHAT?"

"My share, I mean, if I'm not staying on like?"

"Your share. You have it still?"

"Of course I do, I didn't spend any of it, in case . . . you know . . . the guards and everything and a court case and I'd have to give it all back."

"Where is it?"

"It's upstairs in the room."

"In Dublin?"

"No here, back at the house. Under the bed."

"You're not serious."

"But what else would I do with it, Bart? I carry it with me home and back each weekend in a parcel with my clothes."

"And how much is it at all? Your share?"

"I'm afraid it's about four thousand, two hundred pounds," Kev said with his eyes cast down.

Eventually he raised his glance and Bart was smiling at him with pride.

"Isn't that the direct intervention of God?" Bart said to him. Kev would never have seen it like that; however confused his relationship with God was and however non-personal it had become, he couldn't imagine that the Almighty was delighted with such a sum of stolen money arriving under a bed in Rathdoon.

"This solves all our problems," Bart said.

"When Romeo back there went courting Majella the only fly in the ointment was would we have enough to build on a bit at the back. We were afraid it would get a bit crowded with us all on top of each other, and we saw the very thing we wanted, a kind of ready-made extension that they dig foundations for and then sort of plant on top of. Do you follow?"

Kev nodded nervously.

"But Red and I were afraid you were in some kind of financial trouble and we'd better not get ourselves too far into a loan. But here you are, a millionaire. Now we can go ahead, and if you'd like to contribute a bit . . . "

"Yes, well of course I would but don't you think if I'm getting out of their gang I should *offer* them the share back?"

"What kind of criminal are you at all?" roared Bart. "Won't they know immediately you're a ninny if you start a caper like that. You've got to consider that your wages, your share of the deal, now you're meant to be going on to a bigger one, you eejit: you're not meant to be giving them conscience money."

"No."

"And there's no way you can give it to the carpet people or the lavatory makers or the microwave people . . . "

"I wasn't in on the microwave – that's this weekend."

"See?" Bart felt this proved some point. "So what are you going to do with it, wouldn't building up the family home be as good as anything?"

Kev was astonished. No blame, no lecture, no accusation. Sheer hard practical advice, as if he knew the kind of people that Daff and the Pelican were. Because when you thought of it that was EXACTLY the way to go about it. And then he need never see them again.

"I'll give it all to you tonight, Bart," he said eagerly. "Where will we say we got it? Like if anyone asks?"

"You'll keep some of it, put it in the post office, but we'll say nothing to anyone, like you've been doing all your life. We'll get in touch with those people about the extension on Monday. What could be more natural than that country eejits like us would have money in a paper bag under the bed, they'll only be delighted – no VAT, nothing."

Kev was stunned. Saint Bart, in the black economy.

"And thanks to your very generous donation, we'll be able to get the bigger extension, and there'll be plenty of room if Majella produces a brood of Kennedys."

A stone fell off the bridge and into the water and Kev Kennedy didn't jump at all, and his eyes didn't widen with anxiety.

Rupert

He bought a packet of mints because Judy Hickey had told him last week that he reeked of garlic and much as she loved all good herby smells she didn't want to sit cooped up beside a porous sponge of garlic for three hours on a small minibus. Funny, Judy: if he had met her in Dublin, he would never have suspected that she came from home. She wasn't a Rathdoon sort of person. He had told her that once and she had retorted that neither was he – a thin, pale, artistic young Protestant: what could be more unlikely?

But she was wrong. There were handfuls of Protestants in every town in the West; they were as much part of the place as the mountains and the phone boxes and the small beautiful churches with hardly any attendance standing dwarfed by the newer Catholic churches which were bursting at the seams. No use explaining that to Judy, trying to tell her that she was much more unusual, dark and gypsy-like, living in a small gate lodge at the end of the drive from Doon House, growing herbs and working all week in a health food shop in Dublin. In another time she'd have been burned as a witch without any discussion, he had once told her. Judy had said gloomily that the way the country was going it could happen yet, so he shouldn't joke about it.

He smelled of garlic because he had eaten a very good lunch. He always did on a Friday; that was because he wouldn't be back again until late on Sunday night when it was the wrong time to have a meal. So Friday lunchtime was the only opportunity they could get to have anything approaching a relaxed weekend meal before he went back to Rathdoon for the weekend. Of course there *was* the rest of the week but it wasn't quite the same, as there was work next day, and anyway there was something about a weekend that gave you more time – more anticipation. He hated not having his weekends in Dublin. He hated going home on the Lilac Bus.

Rupert had never had an argument with his father in his whole life. And he could remember only three differences of opinion with his mother. Those went back to the time he was away at school and she had written three times to the headmaster to receive assurances that the beds were aired. He knew nobody else in the world who had such a relationship with their parents. Everyone else fought and forgave and loved or hated and stormed and railed or became fiercely protective. Nobody had this polite courteous distance based entirely on gratitude and duty. Nobody else who felt such irritation couldn't express it.

They didn't really need him, that was his whole point, and he wished them well, but he didn't need them either. So why should the pretence be kept up? It made it so much harder on all of them. Not only on Rupert – but maybe it was a little harder on him, he felt, after all their lives were ending. His hadn't really begun and couldn't begin as things were.

There hadn't even been a row when Rupert had decided to give up his law studies. He had been apprenticed to a firm in Dublin, begun his lectures with the Incorporated Law Society and at the same time read for a degree in Trinity. It wasn't a superhuman load – a lot of people did it easily – but Rupert never took to it. Not any of it. The bit he liked best oddly was the office. He was quite happy doing the clerical work, the part that Dee Burke, who worked there now said she hated. Rupert had made few friends in Trinity which surprised him; he thought it would be like school, which had been fine. But it was very different and he felt totally outside it all.

He had come home the weekend he knew he had failed his First Law with a heavy heart. He hadn't tried to excuse himself, he just apologised as if to a kind stranger, and his father accepted the apology as if it had been given by a kind stranger. They had sat one on either side of the table while his mother looked left and right at whoever was speaking.

Rupert said it was a great waste of his father's money and a disgrace to him in his profession. His father had brushed these things aside: heavens no, people often failed their first examination, there was no cause for alarm, some of the greatest lawyers claimed that they had never been showy scholars. No need for any regrets, it should all be written off as part of sowing wild oats, part of getting your freedom. Next year it would be more serious, head in book, down to it, wasn't that right?

On into the night Rupert had talked, saying that he wasn't cut out for it. It wasn't what he wanted. He didn't believe he would love it when he was in his father's office: he didn't love the office he was apprenticed to in Dublin, he only liked the more mechanical parts. He couldn't get interested in the theory of the law or the way it was administered. He was so sorry it had turned out like this, but wasn't it better that they should know now rather than discover later. They agreed logically that it was. They asked him what DID he want. He didn't know; he had been so sure that he would like Trinity, and like studying law, he had never given it much thought before. He liked thinking about the way people lived and their houses and all that. But wasn't it going to be very hard to try and get accepted to study architecture? his father wondered. He didn't mean study it, he didn't know, Rupert said desperately. He would get a job, that's what he'd do. His parents didn't understand this: they thought you had to have a degree to get a job, the kind of job Rupert would want. When he found the position as a junior in the estate agent's they said they were pleased if that's what he wanted. They didn't sound displeased, they sounded remote as they always had been.

His father was remote when he told Rupert that the time had come to get someone else into the office and that if Rupert were absolutely sure that he didn't intend to come into the profession he was going to offer a position to David MacMahon's son. Rupert assured him it would be fine, and got only a minor start when he realised that young MacMahon would have to be offered a partnership and the name of the office would be repainted to read Green and MacMahon. Once or twice they had asked him whether he had thought of coming back to Rathdoon and setting up his own little auctioneering business. There must be plenty of sites being sold and garages and people liked to keep things local. "It might be no harm to get in before Billy Burns sets one up, he's started everything else in the town," his mother had said, but firmly and politely he had assured them that this was not going to happen. He left them in no doubt that his plans involved staying in Dublin. This had happened on the day his mother had said that she wondered whether they should put a new roof on the house or not. Sometimes she felt that the one she had would do for their time and wasn't that all it would be needed for . . . ? Rupert had answered her levelly as if she had been asking no deeper question or making no last desperate plea. He talked of roofs and the value they added to houses and gave the pros and cons as he knew them, bringing himself no more into their plans than if he had been asked by a passing tourist.

His mother asked a bit coyly once or twice if he met any nice girls in Dublin. She didn't ask that any more. He must have given her some fairly firm answers, because he was only twenty-five, an age when you might be assumed to be still meeting girls. If people didn't know that you never met girls, you only met Jimmy.

Rupert's throat tightened just thinking of Jimmy. They had

met for lunch this Friday; it had now become a bit of a ritual. Jimmy had no classes on a Friday afternoon: they had found the boys didn't study too well and had given them games or art or music. So Jimmy could jump into his little car and drive off to meet him. Rupert had noticed with an alarm mixed with pleasure that Dublin was becoming very slap-happy on Friday afternoons anyway, and not just in schools. At the office they did very little business and people seemed to be leaving for home – even if it was just the suburbs – earlier and earlier. If the noise in a nearby pub was anything to go by those particular workers of the world weren't going to do much to change it when they got back to their desks – if they got back. Still it was nice for Rupert. He could take a long lunch hour with no questions asked. They had found a restaurant that both of them liked (not easy as they had such arguments about food), and it was a very happy couple of hours.

Jimmy insisted that he go home every weekend; it was even Jimmy who found the Lilac Bus for him. Jimmy said it was a pity that they couldn't have weekends but it wouldn't be for ever, and since the old man had always been so undemanding wouldn't it only be right to go back to him now in his last few months? And it must be desperate on his mother waiting all week for him: of course he had to go. Jimmy wouldn't even let him pretend he had flu, not even for one weekend. He was very definite about it.

Jimmy was definite about everything, it was part of his charm. He never wondered about anything or deliberated or weighed things up. And if as it turned out sometimes he was utterly wrong, then he was equally definite about that.

"I was all wrong about the man who invented those cats' eyes for the road at night. I was thinking about somebody totally different. I couldn't have been more wrong." Then he would go ahead with the new view. But he had never changed his view about Rupert going home at weekends; that was an absolute.

Jimmy didn't have any home to go off to on a Friday.

Jimmy's home was right there in Dublin. He was the youngest of six, and his two sisters and three brothers had gone exactly the way their father wanted which was into the newspaper vendor business. Some had pitches on good corners, others had roofs over their heads and sold ice creams and birthday cards as well. But Jimmy's father was in the habit of saying gloomily, "There's always one arty farty cuckoo in the nest, one who won't listen to reason." Jimmy had been a bit of a pet when he was a youngster: they all encouraged him at his books, and then to university and into teaching in a very posh school. They made jokes about him being gay but it was never said straight out whether they believed he was or not. Anyone over-educated as they regarded him would have had the same abuse, the accusations of being limp-wristed, the mockery of his clothes, the vain search for an ear ring and the camp clichés from the television: "Ooh Jimmy, you are awful."

But he went there every Wednesday evening. They all called in on the small crowded house; they talked about rivals and which magazine would be seized by the censor as soon as somebody in authority had a look at it. They talked of how the dailies were doing and how there was no point in taking this magazine because it wouldn't survive to a second issue. They told each other how they had long narrow sticks and bet the hands off any kid stealing a comic. Jimmy would join in by asking questions. He always brought a cake, a big creamy one from the nice delicatessen where they often went. His family would have a communal coronary arrest if they knew how much the cake cost. His mother used to say it was a nice piece of cake even though the smallest bit soggy just in the middle. Jimmy would scoop up the bit where the Cointreau or Calvados had concentrated and eat it with a spoon. His brothers said it was a very fair cake, and reminded them of children's trifle.

It would be so easy to have a family like Jimmy's. They asked so little of him, they were so complete in themselves. If Jimmy were to disappear from their lives for ever, he would be spoken of affectionately, but if Rupert were to forgo just one weekend going home on the Lilac Bus it would be a national crisis for the Green family. Sometimes he thought that this was very unfair, but Jimmy would have none of it.

"You're a difficult sensitive plant, Roopo," he'd say. "Even if you had my family, you'd feel threatened and anguished – it's the way things are."

Rupert would laugh, "Don't call me Roopo, it sounds like some exotic bird in the zoo."

"That's what you ARE: like a dark brooding exotic bird that finds almost every climate too difficult for it!"

He had met Jimmy one great lucky day in the office. There was a picture of what they called a "charming unconverted cottage" in the window. It was a bit far out too, not in the more fashionable direction and it could not be described as trendy, even by the most optimistic of those who wrote the descriptions.

Jimmy came in, a slight figure in an anorak, wearing tinted glasses. He had blonde hair that fell over his forehead and he looked a bit vulnerable. Rupert didn't know why he moved over at once to him even though Miss Kennedy was nearer. He didn't feel any attraction to him at that stage – he just wanted to see that he got a fair deal. He had been studying the picture of the cottage, and had an eager smile on his face.

Rupert had told him the good and the bad: the bad being the roof and the distance and awful boulders of rocks in what had been loosely called the garden. He told him the good, which was that it was fairly cheap, that it was nice and private, and that if you had any money now or later there was another building attached to it which was a sort of an outhouse but which could easily be made into another small dwelling. Jimmy listened with growing interest and asked to see it as soon as possible. Rupert drove him out there, and without anything being said they knew they were planning their future as they stood in the wild overgrown rocky ground around the little house and climbed the walls of the outhouse to find that the roof there was perfect.

"It's not handy for where you work," Rupert pointed out, as Jimmy had said where he taught.

"I don't want to live handy to where I work, I want to live miles away. I want to have my own life away from the eyes of the school."

Rupert felt an unreasonable sense of exclusion.

"And will you share it, do you think? That is, if you take it," he had asked.

"I might," Jimmy had said levelly. "I have no plans yet."

He bought the house. He had been saving with a building society for four years and he was considered reliable. The estate agency was pleased with Rupert: they had had the cottage on their books for rather too long. When all the negotiations were over, Rupert felt very lonely. This small smiling Jimmy was going to be off now living his own life in the windswept place. He would build that wall that they had discussed as a shelter, he would do up the second part of the house, paint it white, paint a door bright red maybe, grow some geraniums and get a suitable tenant. It would pay his mortgage. And Rupert would hear no more of it. Or of him.

He phoned on the Friday.

"Rupert, will you help me? I've lost all the fire for the place. I can't SEE it any more, what it's like, what's going to be so great about it. Will you come out and remind me?"

"Yes." Rupert said slowly. "Yes, that's what I'd love to do."

He sat in a kind of trance all that Friday; if people spoke to him he only heard them vaguely. It was all so clear now: the confusions, the guilt, the hope that it would all settle down and sort itself out and that one day a woman would come along who would make him forget all this short-term stuff – which frightened him rather than making him satisfied. But all the time knowing there would be no woman, and not really wanting a woman. But had he read the signs right? Suppose Jimmy was just a charming fellow with nothing on his mind but a good cheery chat with that nice fellow from the estate agent's? Suppose Jimmy said he had a fiancée or some married lady that he wanted to meet in secret. He drove out, noting that it would take him half an hour from door to door should he ever need to go that way again. Jimmy was standing at the gate. Waiting.

He knew it was going to be all right.

And it had been more than all right for three years now. They had done the two little houses up with such love that now they really *did* merit a glowing description on an auctioneer's books. But they would never be for sale. They were separate enough to pretend that they were two dwellings if it were ever needed. But it never was. When Jimmy invited his family out to see the place they all thanked him and said they must get round to it but they never arrived. Rupert didn't press his elderly parents to come to Dublin, and just showed them pictures of his part of the house. And of the garden. They made it all into a giant rockery and knew as much about alpines and rock plants as anyone for miles around. They had a big kitchen with a sink and work area on each side so that they could both cook if they wanted to. Every penny they had went into their little place. They had friends soon, people who came to dinner and admired or offered advice but mainly admired. It was so ideal and they were so happy.

That's why he hated leaving it at weekends. It was on Saturdays that they used to be most peaceful there, often shopping and cooking a meal – not only for Martin and Geoff or other gay friends but for the nice young married couple who lived nearby and who kept an eye on their garden that time they went to Morocco. These were people to relax with. These and one or two people in the estate agency didn't have to have any pretences arranged for them. It was only in Jimmy's school and Rupert's home town that the acting was essential.

Jimmy said it was so ludicrous in the 1980s not to be

able to say that he was gay. And he would have at once it if were remotely possible. But no, apparently the boys' parents would think he had designs on them: they would think he was looking at them speculatively.

"I don't want any of those horrible ink-covered filthy ignorant kids," Jimmy would wail. "I want you, Rupert, my beautiful dark Rupert that I love."

And Rupert would fill up with pleasure and pride that Jimmy could be so natural and open and say all that to him. He tried to say spontaneous things too but they came out with greater difficulty. He was a bit buttoned up as Judy Hickey had once said to him. He wondered often if Judy knew that he was gay. Probably. But it had never been the right time to tell her or to invite her out to see the rock plants and alpines that she would love.

Of course he could tell Judy Hickey: after all, she was a scandal herself in some way, wasn't she? There had been some really murky business years ago. She would be pleased to know there was another Great Secret in Rathdoon. But he could never tell Judy that one of the real reasons he hated so much leaving every Friday for these empty weekends was that he was so afraid Jimmy would find someone else. Or maybe even had found someone else.

At lunch this very Friday he had asked Jimmy what he would do all day Saturday, and there had been no satisfactory answer. Martin and Geoff were having people in for drinks – he would go to that in the evening. He'd mark exercise books, he'd try and fix up the hi-fi which had never been satisfactory. It was all very vague. Suppose, suppose, Jimmy had begun to like somebody else? His heart was cold inside like the unexpected bit you find when you take a loaf out of the freezer and it hasn't properly thawed. He could never tell anyone that fear. Not anyone in the whole world.

It was easy to talk to Judy. She told him about her little herb pillows; he told her all the fuss over the TD with the love nest. They both laughed at that and for some reason that he couldn't quite see it brought her into talking about her own past. He was astounded at her story, a young wife and mother dealing in drugs all those years ago. And the husband doing deals with the law as if he was part of the Wild West. Imagine her not seeing the children, but imagine even more her getting supplies of LSD for the huntin' shootin' fishin' set! And hash! Jimmy would go wild when he heard. He could have listened for ever but suddenly she decided she was boring him and launched into chat with that half-mad Nancy Morris. She had also said that his mother thought about him every day. That couldn't be so. Mother thought about father, and the house, and the vegetable garden and the hens, but mainly father and how she was afraid that young Mr MacMahon didn't have the respect due to the senior partner and founder of the firm. Mother hardly showed any interest in Rupert's life in Dublin which was of course a relief, but it did mean that it was most unlikely that Mother would think about him every day. Surely Judy was being fanciful? She probably hoped no matter what she said her lost children thought of her every day. That was it.

Their house was small and white with clematis growing up over the porch. Jimmy thought that a Protestant solicitor's family would live in a manor house, heavy with creeper and inspiring awe among the peasantry. Rupert had said that only two houses had proper creeper. One was Dr Burke's, which was beautifully kept and one was the old vicarage, which was so neglected it now looked like a huge stone covered with ivy. They had a service each Sunday in Rathdoon in the beautiful church, but had no vicar, no rector; he came out from the big town seventeen miles away and had Matins in Rathdoon, and another, later Matins another fifteen miles down the road. Jimmy was fascinated, but Rupert had never asked Jimmy home to meet the family. Jimmy had asked him to his house many a time. Rupert had gone once and felt awkward even though nobody else had and they had all button-holed him about the price of property.

His mother was waiting just inside the door. That always annoyed him too and he got annoyed with himself over the very annoyance. Why shouldn't she wait to stop him ringing or knocking and disturbing his father's sleep. But it always made him think she had been standing waiting for his shadow to fall through the glass panels. He said goodnight with a much lighter tone than he felt, and braced himself. The soft leather of the magnificent jacket touched the back of his neck. It was Jimmy's birthday present to him. A few days early but Jimmy said it would cheer him up for the weekend. Dee Burke had been right, they did cost a fortune. Again the niggling worry: how had Jimmy been able to spend that much money even if it was a second? Put these doubts away, Rupert, he told himself firmly. Jimmy is good and true. Why pour vinegar onto it all with your stupid suspicions. Jimmy is at home tonight marking books and looking at television, Jimmy is not in a bar in town cruising someone. Why destroy EVERYTHING?

"He's very well, very clear," his mother whispered delightedly.

"What?"

"Your father. He's very clear. He's awake; he asked several times what time would the Lilac Bus be in. Every time he heard anything change gear on the corner, he said 'Is that the bus?' "

Rupert put his carrier bag down on the hall floor. "That's great Mother, that's really great," he said with heavy heart and went up the little stairs slowly to see the man with the head like a skull and the skin like cling-film. The man he had never been able to talk to in his life.

It was a sunny Saturday but his father's room was darkened and the dim light hurt his eyes. His mother was bottling fruit downstairs. Jimmy said Catholics never bottled fruit or preserved eggs – it was something their religion didn't go along with. Jimmy had told him more lies about Roman Catholicism than he ever believed anyone could invent. He had always been brought up carefully to

146

respect it at a distance by his parents, and even though they thought it definitely held the people back they were impressed by the piety and the crowds going to Mass. His parents had gone to Galway to see the Pope. Jimmy said that his parents had made a small fortune the weekend the Pope arrived since the whole of Dublin wanted to buy every newspaper twice in case they missed anything.

Back at home in the cottage, Jimmy would be drinking freshly brewed coffee and reading the *Irish Times*. Then he might go out to the garden and do some transplanting. September was the month to move the evergreens if you wanted to change the plan a bit. But no, Jimmy would wait for him to come back for that. Maybe he would be puzzling over the hi-fi. Please may he not be driving into town just because he's bored; please may he meet nobody at lunch over a drink and smoked salmon sandwich.

"You're very good to come down every weekend," his mother said suddenly as if she could read the homesickness for his real place written all over his eyes. "Your father really does like talking to you. Do you notice that? Can you see it?"

Jimmy had begged him not to cross the whole of Ireland and then have a row. How could Jimmy understand that there were NEVER rows, and there never would be. Well, a coldness then, Jimmy would say. If you are going to go to all that trouble, it's silly to balls up your weekend: if you're making the gesture, make it properly.

"I think he *does* seem to like talking," Rupert said. "It doesn't tire him too much does it?"

"No, he plans all week what he's going to say to you. Sometimes he asks me to write it down, or just headings. I want to talk to Rupert about this, he'll say, and I write it down. Often he forgets what it was he was going to say about it, but it's there at the time."

Rupert nodded glumly.

"Like he was going to ask you about those flats you sell in blocks; he was very interested in how they work out the leasehold. He said that there was never any of that in the conveyancing he had to do. But all he asked me to write down was 'Block of Flats,' you see, and then he couldn't remember last week what it was he wanted to say about them."

"I see," Rupert said, trying to sound more sympathetic than he was afraid he might appear.

"But this week, he seems very much brighter and more aware, doesn't he?" she was pleading.

"Yes, much more. Oh indeed. He was talking about this house here and what we would say if we had it on an auctioneer's books. I was giving him funny descriptions and he smiled a bit at it."

Rupert's mother was pleased. "Good, he hasn't smiled a lot. That's nice."

"Why don't you have a bit of time off, Mother, when I'm here. Why can't you go into town, maybe, you'd like that. I can keep an eye on father and be here if he wants anything."

"No no, I want you to enjoy yourself," she said.

"But really Mother, I mean I'm not doing anything anyway." He shrugged. "I might as well look after father and let you have a few hours to yourself." He meant it generously, but he knew it had come out all wrong.

"But you're home for the weekend," she cried. "I wouldn't want to miss that by going off to the town. I can do that any day: Mrs Morris or young Mary Burns, Billy's wife, would sit with him. No, I want to get value out of your being here."

"Sure. Of course," he said, appalled at his own insensitivity. Jimmy would never in a million years have said anything like that. Jimmy would have brought life and laughter into the house the moment he got back. Jimmy. Oh Jimmy.

They had lunch, the kind of lunch that only his mother could serve: endless preparation and toasting of bread and cutting of crusts and spreading of cheese and slicing of tomatoes. And yet it was nothing – it managed to be both stodgy and insubstantial. If only she would let him cook. But then he had never asked her. Perhaps it might be giving something away to say that he could have made them a light and delicious lunch in a quarter the time. It was his own fault like everything.

His father struggled all afternoon. And Rupert struggled back.

Sometimes his mother was there, sewing. She was always making little things for her sister who was married to a vicar and who always needed things for parish sales. His father would struggle and concentrate. His efforts to please meant that he could even be re-routed back to his own old days as a solicitor coming first to the town, when things were different and better. There was a time when his father had been happy to ramble through the times gone by. But not now: it was as if he was determined to show a guest in his eyes that he *was* interested in whatever kind of strange thing the guest did for a living. All afternoon Rupert's soul was crying out, "It's all RIGHT father. Look, can't you rest: I have an okay life and I wish you and mother well but why do we go through all this meaningless chat. There is nothing to say any more."

The sun was almost going down when he could bear it no more; he said he had promised Judy Hickey he would do something for her and he had better dash over to her.

"A brave woman, Judy Hickey – she held her head high in this place for two decades," his father said in a surprisingly strong voice.

"Yes, well, why not?" Rupert was defensive. "She got a harsh punishment."

"She took it, and she didn't run away and hide. She stepped down from being lady of the manor and lived in the gate lodge."

"And lost her children," Rupert's mother added. "That was the worst bit."

"Yes, well, I won't be long." He felt he could breathe again when he was out in the air; he left the square and went off towards the gate lodge of the big Doon house.

Judy was lying curled up like a cat. She wasn't pleased to see him – in fact she nearly sent him back straight away. She was like Jimmy really but without the persuasive charm: Jimmy made it seem reasonable; Judy made it seem like a duty.

But she meant it: she got up and stretched and said she was going to go out and walk in her husband's wood. Jack Hickey's wood she called it. She said he should talk about anything, anything to show his father that he was trying too.

But what could he say? He couldn't tell him that his heart was tearing with the barbed wire of jealousy in case his male lover might have been unfaithful. Then NOBODY could tell a father that about a lover of any sex. But Rupert was worse off: he couldn't talk about his life, about the beautiful gentians that he and Jimmy had planted and how the willow gentian had burst into a whole pool of dark blue flowers last July and they had taken photographs of each other admiring it. He found it hard to talk about the garden without mentioning Jimmy because the two were twined together, like the house, like cooking, like holidays and reading and laughing and the things people did for heaven's sake.

Annoyed with Judy for being short with him, he walked home. He passed the Kennedys' shop and saw a big handsome girl being ushered in. The red-headed Kennedy boy, Eddie, was looking at her with a foolish grin: they must be courting. She was very attractive; how simple life would have been if only he had been born to court a big handsome girl who would bring life and laughter into his quiet house.

Suddenly he thought of Jimmy in the house. Jimmy pausing at the door to touch the clematis and cup it in his hands with admiration. Jimmy saying to Rupert's mother that she should sit down and put her feet up and let her big ugly son and himself make the meal for a change. Jimmy telling Rupert's father tales of the boys' school where he taught, and the fees and the extras and the awful school concerts. Jimmy walking casually down the road with him to Ryan's for a drink before dinner while the carbonade was in the oven. Jimmy would lighten their house better than any strapping girl from a well-to-do farm outside town.

"I was just thinking," he said to his mother when she let him in the door again as if she had been hovering. "Could I bring a friend home next weekend?"

After that it was easy. His mother said she was glad that she had got good notice because she would clear out the guest room. It had been something she had meant to do for a long time but never had the heart somehow. And his father said that it would be very interesting to meet someone who taught in that school because he had known a lot of people in his time who had been there and they were all united in never having a good word to say for it but having done extremely well as a result of being there.

Then a sudden shock. Suppose Jimmy didn't want to come?

"I hope he'll be able to make it; I didn't think of asking him," he stammered.

"Why don't you ring him?" his mother suggested. His mother. Who made trunk calls as one might try to get in touch with another planet. Cautiously and without much hope of success.

"God, isn't that lovely to hear you?" Jimmy said.

"I'm ringing from home," said Rupert.

"Well, I hope so. I did think sometimes you went off to exotic places without me, but I decided to trust you." Jimmy's laugh was warm. Rupert swallowed.

"It's lovely here this weekend and I was wondering . . . I was wondering . . . ."

"Yes?"

"I was wondering if you'd like to come down next week and stay, you know?"

"I'd love to.'"

There was a pause.

"You would? You would, Jimmy?"
"Sure I thought you'd never ask," Jimmy said.

Celia

Her friend Emer used to call it the Dancing Bus. All over Dublin people got on buses on Friday night to go home to great dances in the country. It had been a revolution, they said – culchies choosing to go home because the crack was better there than in Dublin. And they had the advantages of a bit of freedom in the city during the week and not losing touch with the home place either.

Celia laughed at the thought of her bus being a Sweetheart Special. She told Emer when they had cups of tea in the day room about the cast that turned up at a quarter to seven every week. Emer had sighed in envy. It sounded great, a nice spin across to the west, a weekend with no washing and housecleaning and trying to tell the three teenagers that there wasn't enough money for anything and trying to tell her husband who had been out of work for three years that there was plenty of money for everything. Emer had a sister married in the town that was seventeen miles from Rathdoon. Wouldn't it be lovely to go off there once in a while? Oh Lord, she'd love it.

And so that's what happened. Celia had to work weekends, one in every four. So she gave her place on the bus to Emer. It had suited them all, and Emer said her family in Dublin were so grateful to see her back on a Sunday night that they never complained about anything, they just made her a coffee and said they'd missed her. Of course Celia did go to the dances at one time, and they were great altogether: you got a first-rate band to come to a place where the people drove in for miles and there would always be a big crowd. She used to dance with Kev Kennedy's brother, Red, sometimes, but she much preferred Bart, the eldest of that family. He was so solid and reliable. You never quite knew what he was thinking but he was always there. In fact you never had to ASK him to help, he seemed to know when it was necessary and turn up. Emer said he sounded a very suitable sort of man indeed, but Celia thought not. She said he wasn't interested in settling down and she wasn't going to set her sights on another one who was a permanent bachelor. She'd had enough trouble getting over the first. Emer had sighed supportively and wondered why as a married woman she was trying to encourage others to join the club. It certainly wasn't what it was cracked up to be, and in many ways it wasn't much good at all.

But Celia only laughed at her. Emer was thirty-eight and sounded tough and cynical but deep down she would die for that handsome, whinging husband of hers and those tall rangy kids who got bigger and needed more clothes every time you looked at them. Celia wasn't going to be put off love and marriage by any of Emer's protests; it was what she wanted. Not urgently, not immediately, not at any price, but she wanted it sometime. Despite what she had seen of it in her own family.

She could hardly remember a day at home when there hadn't been some kind of a row. A lot of them were in public too because if the whole of Rathdoon was coming into the pub from eleven o'clock in the morning on, then they would have to be aware of the shouts and the disagreements and the sight of Mr or Mrs Ryan coming flushed with anger from the back room into the bar and serving a pint, only to disappear again and fight the point further. Celia had often heard that children grew anxious and withdrawn when their parents fought in the home. But that's not what happened to the Ryans. They grew up and went away, that was all. As soon as they were able to get out, out they got. Her eldest sister had joined a band of Australian nuns who had come to Ireland looking for vocations. Looking for very young vocations, since Celia's sister had only been sixteen. But the offer of further education had been attractive as well. She wrote home from time to time incomprehensible letters of places and things that were never explained. Then the boys had gone too. Harry to Detroit and Dan to Cowley in England. They wrote rarely, hard sorts of letters with a kind of graspingness they never had as youngsters – how a bar in Ireland must be a gold mine now. Harry had read in Detroit that Ireland was booming since the Common Market, and Dan had been told in Cowley that having a publican's license in the west of Ireland was like having a licence to print money. These letters hurt Celia: there was much more than a hint, there was a direct statement that Celia and her mother were doing very nicely out of the family business, thank you. When she saw how things really were she felt she should laugh, but before she laughed she should weep.

Five years ago when her father died people said that at least one blessing was that Kate Ryan had always been more or less running the business single-handed and so there'd be no doubt at all that she'd be able to carry on. It wasn't like some establishments where the wife had always been in the background. No, poor Kate had been managing on her own while the husband drank down at one end of the bar with his own little circle.

And poor Kate had carried on for a good bit. In the summer she'd hire a young fellow to wash glasses and there was always Bart Kennedy to give a hand if things got very busy. No, she was fine. There was no shortage of customers, and mercifully drink wasn't the kind of thing that came and went in fashions – people always loved drink. Apart from the first week of Lent, the custom was always steady and at weekends it was roaring. There was no opposition, and you'd never get another licence for a place as small as this.

Rathdoon was unusual in that it had only one pub; other places might have had three. There had been talk once that Billy Burns was thinking of applying for a licence; he had been interested in buying a place about twenty miles away and asking to transfer that licence to Rathdoon, but nothing had come of it.

Celia had been thinking about Billy Burns during the day for some reason. She had woken with that silly tune on her mind, "Where have you been all the day, Billy Boy, Billy Boy?" and she thought it fitted Mikey's brother down to the ground. Mikey was such an innocent old eejit, and there was something a bit too smart about Billy. Nothing to do with his setting up another pub or not. In fact if he did that might be a solution to a lot of their problems. If her mother's pub went downhill due to legitimate competition that would be an honourable way out. If her mother drank Ryan's into the ground that was a less honourable way altogether.

But you couldn't say anything even vaguely like this to Celia's mother. Other people were hitting it a bit hard these days, other people were making fools of themselves and running up debts: there were men in Rathdoon who had big pores in their noses and red and blue veins in their cheeks from drink; there were women in Rathdoon who went into the big town seventeen miles away to do the shopping, but Kate Ryan could tell you that it was little shopping they did except half a dozen half-bottles hidden under the teatowels or whatever they bought as an excuse. Half bottles were easier to hide and they were easier to dispose of. Kate Ryan could tell you of those who came in at night for just one drink, Mrs Ryan, and she had seen them topping it up from their handbags. They didn't want to be seen ordering more than the one. But Celia's mother would have no tales of a woman who didn't even have to hide it because she had it there on her own shelves, and she was surrounded by it as her way of earning a living for twelve hours a day.

It had been such a shock the first time she saw her mother

drunk. Mam had been the one who didn't and Da had been the one who did. It was like left and right and black and white. To hear those slurred words, to have to cope with an inarticulate argument – Celia had been quite flustered and not at all the calm Nurse Ryan that could cope with anything on her corridor. The next day her mother had made great excuses, frightening excuses. It was food poisoning: she had eaten some of that chicken paste out of a jar, she was going to write to the manufacturers and enclose the label. Not only had it made her sick several times during the night but it had also affected her mind in some way. She couldn't remember clearly, she couldn't piece everything together. When Celia said agreeably enough that the chicken paste might well have been bad but it was probably the drink that made her forget the night before, she flew into a rage, one of those real rows like there used to be when Da was alive. It was NOT drink. Could Celia kindly tell her what drink she was referring to? Had Celia seen her mother sitting down to have a drink even once last night? Celia shrugged. She thought it might have been just this one time. Let it pass.

Three weeks later she came home for the weekend, and her mother was mixing up the gin and the vodka, forgetting to take the money from people and letting the pints overflow while she went to deal with someone else. It was then that Celia decided she had better book herself onto the Lilac Bus and come home every weekend that she could. This had been going on for a year now and her mother was getting worse and worse. And the really bad thing was that she wouldn't admit it, not for one moment. Not even to herself.

In the hospital Celia had seen dozens – more than dozens, probably hundreds – of people who were trying to help people who wouldn't help themselves. There had been endless conversations about old men who wouldn't go into sheltered accommodation and had set fire to their kitchens three times and old women who had broken their hips over and over because they wouldn't ask anyone to help them across a street. There were shrivelled anorexics who wouldn't eat, there were ashen-faced coronary patients who had insisted on doing overtime in stress-filled jobs and eating huge meals filled with cholesterol. There were women worn out with the fourteenth pregnancy, there were the mothers of the schoolchildren who had overdosed, there were the wives of the men whose livers had packed up despite a hundred arguments that alcohol was poisoning them slowly to certain death. Always she had sounded sympathetic, always she had appeared to understand. But inside there was a bit of her which said that they couldn't have tried hard enough. If Celia had a daughter who was desperately unhappy at school and who had lost four stone in weight, she wouldn't hang around – she'd try to cope with it. If she had a father who couldn't cope, she'd have him to live with her. Only now was she beginning to realise that it was not to be so simple. People had minds of their own. And her mother's mind was like a hermetically sealed box in the vault of a bank.

Emer had been in high good humour: she had won a hundred pounds on the hospital draw. Each week they all had to buy a ticket for the building fund. It cost fifty pence, and they *had* to buy it – there wasn't any choice. Three hundred fifty pences aded up to £150 and every second week the prize was £50 and every other one it was £100. It kept people interested and that small weekly contribution to the building fund was assured. Even if you were going to be on holidays you had to give someone else your sub. The winning ticket was announced on a Friday afternoon by number and you went to Wages to collect the prize. Emer was going to say nothing about it at home. Not one word. They would never hear. They would want jeans, they'd want a holiday, they'd think you could go on a holiday for a hundred quid. They'd want to go to Macdonalds every night for a month, they'd want a video. Her husband would say it should go into the building society, it should be saved in case he never worked again. No, much better to keep it for herself. She and Celia would have a night out next week. Celia had laughed at her affectionately. "Sure," she had said. "People do what they want in the end, isn't that what you always say?"

She knew that what Emer would want despite all the protestations of independence and keeping the money to herself was totally different. She would want to arrive home this Friday night bursting with the news. She would want to send out for chicken and chips and plan endless treats which would indeed include jeans and a bit saved to please her anxious husband and a promise to look into the economics of a down payment on a video. That's what Emer would want and that's what she would do in the end. They both knew it.

And if Celia had a husband and kids she hoped that's what she would want too. Otherwise what was the point of the whole thing?

She was tired. It had been a long day. In other hospitals they worked twelve hour shifts: eight in the morning till eight at night. Celia thought she'd be ready to strangle some of the patients, most of the visitors and all of the staff if they had to have that routine. It had been quite enough to have eight hours today. A young woman had become desperately upset because at visiting time her a brother, a priest, had said that he was saying a special Mass for her in their house. He had thought she would be pleased; she had thought that this meant it was the end. Then her husband told the priest that he had a neck to come in and upset the wife and there was a row of such proportions that everyone in the ward stopped talking to their own visitors and began to listen. Celia had been called. She pulled the curtains round the bed, she organised some light sedation, she explained in a crisp cool voice that the woman's diagnosis had been entirely optimistic, that nothing was being hidden from her or from anyone. She said that since priests had the power to say the Mass, what could be more natural than he would say one in the family home as a thanksgiving for her recovery so far and a hope that it would continue?

She also said with a particularly pointed look at the priest that it was a pity some people couldn't explain things sensibly without using voices laden with doom and ritual, and have some sensitivity about people's association of having Masses said with being very ill indeed. Then with a reprimanding glance at the husband she said that the whole point of a visiting hour was for the patient to be made more comfortable and happy and not to be plunged into the middle of a huge family row with accusations being hurled for the whole ward to hear. They were all younger than her except the priest, and he was probably under thirty. They took it very well and nodded their apologies to her and to each other. She drew the curtains open again and busied herself around the ward until she was sure they were all properly calm again. When the priest and the husband had gone she sat with the woman and held her hand and told her not to be an eejit: priests would want to say a Mass in a house at the drop of a hat. And after all it was their life. If they didn't believe it was important, who did? It was only the rest of the world, Celia explained, who thought that Masses and God were only brought in when all else had failed. For priests they were there all the time. She hit the right note exactly and the woman was laughing by the time she left the ward.

Would that it were going to be so easy at home.

Last weekend Bart Kennedy had let slip that he had been there several nights during the week as well as the weekends. She was alarmed. She and Bart never spoke of the reason for him being there. He never said that her mother was drunk, he would say she needed a bit of a hand. He never said that her mother had insulted one of the customers, he would say there had been a bit of a barney but it was probably all sorted out now. She had asked him to

162

take wages for himself, and he had laughed and said not at all. He was only helping out and how could he go and sign on if he was getting a regular salary? He assured her that he took the odd pint for himself and offered one to a friend occasionally but it was peanuts and couldn't go on. Emer wondered had he perhaps any hopes of marrying into the establishment, but Celia said that was nonsense – Bart wasn't the type. Nothing funny about him, mind you, but just one that would never marry. Don't forget, Celia knew all about those: she had served her time for five years on a hopeless cause. She could spot them a mile off now.

But enough: she wasn't going to think of that fellow any more. That was all behind her and at least the humiliations weren't known in Rathdoon. It was to another town that she had followed him hopefully at weekends, thinking that there was much more to it than there was, being there, being available; eventually because it seemed the one thing he was sure he wanted she had slept with him. That was what he had called it but there was no sleeping involved: it was guilt for fear of discovery, and not very much pleasure for either of them. She hadn't lost him because she had been too easy to get; she hadn't lost him at all because he was never hers to lose; he had no intention of disturbing the very even pattern of his life by a wife and house and children. No no, no, he would stay on with his parents while they lived and maybe with a sister later. There would always be girls – girls now and later women – who would believe that they had the secret and the key to unlock his independence. No, Celia could write a book on the Irish bachelor if she wanted to, but she hadn't time: she HAD to sort it out this weekend, otherwise she'd better leave the hospital and come home. It wasn't fair on everyone else in Rathdoon.

She was glad that Kev Kennedy was a little bit ahead of her. That meant that he would sit beside Mikey. Tonight she was not in the mood for Mikey's jokes; some evenings she could take a few and then turn to her own thoughts but there was too much on her mind, and Mikey was so easily hurt. It was good not to have this battle between offending him or going mad herself. She slipped easily in beside Tom the driver. He leaned over her and slammed the door shut.

"It's only twenty to seven. I have you all very well trained," he said and they all laughed with him as the bus went out into the traffic and headed for home.

Tom was a fine companion. He always answered agreeably and gave long answers if he were in the mood to chat and short ones if he weren't. The silences were companionable. He never talked to the people behind because it distracted him, and he liked the person sitting beside him to tell him if it was all clear on the left as they nosed onto main roads from side roads. Much nicer than the rest of the FitzGeralds up in the craft shop, but then it was silly to expect families to be the same. Look at Billy Burns: he'd buy and sell Mikey a dozen times before breakfast. Nancy Morris – there was something wrong with her, Celia thought. She had a very fixed look, a look that really was fixed on nothing. Celia had seen it in hospital sometimes. Nancy was as different from that laughing Deirdre, her sister in America, as she was different to a Martian. And there was poor Kev, Bart's young brother behind her there in the bus. And possibly she was different to her own brothers and sister. At the thought of her own family her brow darkened. Why would none of them do a thing to help? How had it happened? She *could* write them a round robin: "Dear Maire and Harry and Dan, Sorry to have to tell you but Mam is hitting the bottle worse than ever Dad did. What will we do? Looking forward to hearing by return from New South Wales, Cowley, Oxfordshire, and Detroit, Michigan, Your loving sister, Celia, Dublin." That was the point: Dublin. It was only up the road as far as they were concerned, and she wasn't married, that was even more the point wasn't it? If she had been a wife then none of them would have expected her to abandon that and look after her mother, no matter how near she was. But being a nurse, an

164

angel of mercy, helping the sick and earning her living . . . that would be written off.

And what's more they wouldn't understand, any of them. Maire would write from Woolowogga or wherever she had gone on a course – she was always going to ludicrou places on courses – and she would say it was Blessed to give and Blessed to help. Great. Harry would write from Detroit and say she must do what she thought was best as she was the one on the ground. He would add something about it being a nice tidy living for her, and probably put in a really sensitive bit about not wanting his share out of the family business yet. Dan would write, he might even ring from England: he'd encourage her like mad to go home, he'd say that nursing wasn't a REAL career or anything, and that it was all for the best. His bit of tact might be to hope that now she was known as the landlady of a pub in all but name perhaps Celia might get a few offers of marriage. She was only twenty-six, why had they written her off in three countries? She was their baby sister, she remembered them as big and strong and great fun, but in their letters and their rare appearances they were selfish and they were strangers. And they thought of her as an old maid.

"Do your family drive you mad?" she asked Tom as they had just overtaken a huge dangerous-looking lorry that seemed about to shed everything it had on everything that was near it.

"Oh yes, of course they do," Tom said. "I mean that IS what drives people mad actually, families. It's not strangers in the street or the Bomb or the economy, it's always their relations."

"Or love, I suppose, or lack of it?" Celia was impersonal, interested in talking about ideas. So was Tom. That's why they found their chats easy and never found their long silences threatening.

"Yes, love, but love usually involves some idea of family: you love someone, you want her to be your wife; she won't, you go mad. That's family. You hate your wife, you don't love her any more, you wish she'd fly off on the next space shuttle. That's family."

Celia laughed. "God you'd be great in one of those family counselling places with psychiatrists and all."

"I'm always surprised they never asked me in on one," said Tom, and they didn't speak for another fifty miles.

She was glad to get out and stretch. She had heard of other buses where they got stuck into a pub like this one for a real session and maybe it would be an hour and half before people got back on the road. But Tom Fitzgerald ruled his Lilac Bus very firmly, it was time to visit the Ladies' and a very quick drink. There really wasn't even time for a coffee because they always took such ages to make it in pubs, and indeed in Ryan's of Rathdoon they wouldn't make it at all.

"What'll you have Celia?" Dee had a knack of getting to the counter quickest and an even better knack of getting served. Celia had a bottle of Guinness and a few words. Dee had never changed, not since she was a schoolgirl bursting with pride at her new uniform and coming into the bar to show it off to the Ryans. She had been everywhere to show it off, and everyone had given her a lemonade, or a bar of chocolate or even half a crown. Nobody had anything but good wishes for the doctor's daughter off to her posh convent boarding school. Dr Burke was part of every life and death in Rathdoon, nobody would have a jealous thought about his children and what they had. Who would deserve it more?

She slipped Mikey some ointment that they used up in the hospital to ease bedsores. She didn't want to let Dee see her in case it was thought that she might be trying to improve on the doctor, but Dee would probably never think that in a million years. She was a grand girl with a very infectious laugh, and of course she had the patience of Job that she could talk to Nancy Morris so animatedly about Nancy's boring job and her endless tales of Mr This the consultant and Mr That the consultant. How did Dee put up with it and even look interested and remember their bloody names? The ten minutes were up and they were back in the dark comfort again.

She saw that Tom had tapes in the van; she had never noticed them before.

"Is that a player as well as a wireless?" she asked with interest when they were on the road again.

"Yes, do you wonder I have to guard this vehicle with my life? All I own is tied up in her," he laughed.

"You don't play any, while we're driving?"

"No. I thought about it: everyone would have a different taste and I wouldn't want to inflict my choice on all of you."

"Oh, it would have to be yours, would it?" Celia threw back her head of thick brown hair, laughing at him. "Where's the democratic bit then? Why couldn't everybody choose their own, even bring one each week?"

"Because if I had to hear any more of the Nashville sound than I already hear by accident in my life, I think I'd drive off the road and into the deepest bog that would close over us," he said.

"Let's have no music then," Celia said agreeably and they drove on thinking their own thoughts. Celia was wondering what time she would catch her mother at the most receptive. There must be *some* moments in the day when the unfortunate woman was not suffering from a hangover or withdrawal or had got stuck into it again. There must be a time – late morning maybe – when she could ask Bart to man the place. Not that anyone came in much on a Saturday until it was well into lunchtime. She could always put CLOSED on the door, Father Reilly put closed on the presbytery for heaven's sake when he simply had to have an hour to himself, or maybe it was for some poor divil that couldn't be disturbed. That was it, no more drawing on poor Bart. Anyway he liked to work with Judy Hickey during the daytime when she was home for the weekend. She could put CLOSED on the door for an hour or two, but apart from chaining her mother by both wrists and ankles how was she going to get her to stay and listen to the very unwelcome view that she was now incapable of managing her own pub and must get herself into an alcoholic unit before it was too late? It was gone beyond false promises now, and assurances and little games. Celia had been present when a surgeon told a forty-two year old man last month that he had terminal cancer and had less than two months to live. This is what it felt like again. That sense of dread and half hoping the world would end before you had to say it. Of course it had turned out very oddly in the hospital; they had thought the shock might be intense and that was why Celia was there as part of a back-up. But he had been very quiet, the man, and said, "Is that a fact?" They had stood dumbfounded, Celia, the great surgeon and the anaesthetist. Then the man had said, "And I never went to America. Imagine in my whole life I never saw America. Isn't it ridiculous in this day and age." He had said that several times before he died; it seemed to disturb him more than death itself and leaving his wife and three young children.

Suppose her mother were to say something equally unexpected like that she had been wondering was this what was wrong with her, and she would like to go at once as a voluntary patient to some kind of place that would dry her out. Stop thinking like Alice in Wonderland, Celia told herself sternly. You're a grown-up, it's no use shutting your eyes wishing things would happen.

"There's a lot of rags tied to a bush coming up now. I think it's a holy well or a wishing tree or something," Tom said suddenly. "Maybe we should all get out and tie our shirts to it," Celia said. They passed it, and indeed there were ribbons and what looked like holy pictures pinned onto it.

"I never saw that before, and all the times we must have driven past it," Celia said, looking back over her shoulder. She thought she saw Dee Burke crying, her face was working in that sort of way a child's does to keep off the sobs. But Nancy Morris was yammering on as usual so there couldn't be anything really wrong.

"I never saw it before. Maybe it's a new saint; you know the way they get crossed off like St Philomena, maybe one got put on."

"Why DID St Philomena get crossed off, I wonder?" asked Celia.

"I don't know, maybe they found her out," Tom grinned. "I know my sister Phil was very annoyed indeed at the time, she felt it was an attack of some sort."

"Oh yes, Phil, that would be her name. How is Phil by the way? I haven't seen her for a while."

"She's fine," Tom said shortly.

Celia went back to the tree for conversation. "Are they pagan or are they religious, I wonder?" she said.

"A mixture, I think." He was still short.

Celia thought about the tree. Wouldn't it be great to go there and pray to some saint who had a special interest in drunken mothers, leave an offering or whatever they left and then go home and discover that it had worked. Bart Kennedy would be serving behind the bar and her mother would be sitting with a packed suitcase and face full of optimism.

"See you during the weekend," Tom said with a friendly smile.

She nodded. He had been a bit moody tonight, she thought. She didn't mind their stops and starts normally, in fact she liked it. But tonight she had wanted to talk. Actually what she had really wanted was Emer. You could say anything to Emer and you knew she would think about it but she wouldn't bring it out again on every occasion and ask you how you felt about it. Emer would give you advice but not be annoyed if you didn't take it. "Everyone does what they want to in the end" she would say. She wasn't as specific when it came to knowing how to convince someone else to do the right thing. Or the best thing. Celia had long discussions with her over this. Did you wire the jaws of fat kids who were compulsive eaters? Did you have medical cards for smokers and only those who were certified as having good strong lungs and no trace of emphesema would be allowed to buy a packet – they'd have to show the card first. That would save life wouldn't it? Celia might suggest. Emer would shrug. Temporarily only: the child with the wired jaw would wait eagerly until the contraption was removed; the smoker would get the cigarettes somehow or smoke butts. But then why were drugs banned? Why not just sell heroin by the kilo in Quinnsworth and be done with it. Those who wanted to kill themselves would and there would be no drugs racket and pushers and people having to turn to prostitution or theft for it.

Emer said that drugs were different: they were poison, they killed. You wouldn't sell arsenic or strychnine would you?

What about alcohol: that killed, they had seen enough rotted livers to know that; they could see the slow death around them. Emer said that if Celia felt as strongly as that she shouldn't own a pub, and she should have a temperance banner. Then they would both have a bottle of Guinness and talk about something else. But she was such a comfort; no wonder that her handsome husband and her three giant children were always waiting so eagerly for her to come home from work. And she wasn't a Superwoman either. There were bad times and low times in Emer's life as well as in everyone else's. That's why she was so good to talk to.

"Goodnight," she nodded, and added "Thanks for getting us here." She didn't want to be curt with Tom just because he hadn't been like Emer! That would be unfair.

"Best to the West, as Mikey would say," Tom laughed.

"Don't encourage him – he has enough catchphrases already." She went in the door and knew from the loud greeting that her mother called across the bar that it was going to be a long hard hour and a half. She put her bag in the kitchen, she hung up her jacket and came out quietly to stand beside Bart Kennedy who patted her on the arm as she wordlessly began to pull the pints.

Her mother shouted for two hours when the pub eventually closed. She sat at one of the tables and hurled abuse as Celia methodically emptied the ashtrays and wiped the surfaces. She would NOT be patronised in her own pub, she cried, she would not have Celia coming off the bus and taking over as if she owned the place. Celia did NOT own the place and in fact the place would never be hers. She hoped that Celia knew this. She had made a will with that nice young Mr MacMahon in Mr Green's office, and she had said that after her death the pub should be sold and the money divided equally in four and shared out between Maire and Harry and Dan and Celia. So now. Celia said nothing. She washed the glasses under hot water first, then under cold, then turned them upside down to drain on a plastic grid: that way the air got at them from all angles and dried them without smears.

Her mother had a brandy bottle on the table beside her. Celia made no attempt to touch it. She just moved past her and locked the door. The place was now ready for the next day. She gulped a bit at the thought of the conversation she was going to have in the morning when the closed sign would appear on Ryan's door for the first time since her father's funeral.

"Aren't you going to have the common manners to say goodnight, Miss High and Mighty?" her mother called.

"Goodnight Mam," said Celia as she went up the narrow stairs wearily to the small white bedroom with the iron bed. She lay awake for a while. Long enough to hear her mother stumbling up the stairs and hitting off the chest of drawers on the landing. She must have known it was there: it had been there for thirty-eight years, all her married life.

It was very sunny, too sunny. Celia woke with a jump. The curtains had been pulled back, and there was her mother with a cup of tea.

"I thought you might like this, after your week's work,

and you must have stayed up late last night doing the glasses." The voice was steady enough and the hand wasn't shaking as it passed the tea-cup and saucer.

Celia sat up and rubbed her eyes. "You were with me when I washed the glasses," she said.

"I know, I know, of course," her mother was flustered, she hadn't remembered. "Yes well, naturally, but thanks for . . . um . . . organising it all the same."

There was no smell of drink but Celia realised that she must have had a cure, maybe a vodka. That's why she was able to cope. She had smartened herself up too, combed her hair and worn a dress with a white collar. Apart from her eyes which looked terrible, Mrs Ryan didn't cut too bad a figure at all.

This might be the time. Celia swung her legs out of the bed, and took a great swig of the tea.

"Thanks Mam. Listen, I wanted to say something to you. I've been trying to get a good time . . ."

"I have a kettle on downstairs; I'll come back up to you when I have a minute."

She was gone. There was no kettle on. Celia got up and dressed quickly. She decided against jeans and put on a skirt and blouse and a big wide belt. It made her look more authoritative, more nurse-like in a way. There was no sign of her mother in the kitchen. Where could she have gone? There was a sound of scrubbing out the side entrance, and there was Mrs Ryan on hands and knees with bucket and scrubbing brush working away.

"I was noticing this last night: it's in a very bad way, we mustn't let the place go to rack and ruin around us." She was sweating and puffing. Celia let her at it. She went back into the kitchen and made more tea. Eventually her mother had to come back in.

"There, that's much better," she said.

"Good," said Celia.

"I saw that Nancy Morris, a proper little madam that one. 'Hallo Mrs Ryan' if it suits her, and wouldn't give you the time of day if it didn't. I pretended I didn't hear her. She has her mother scalded coming home every weekend."

"I'm sure," Celia said. Mrs Ryan's jaw dropped.

"Oh not like you. I mean it's grand that you come home, and you're such a help."

"I'm glad you think so this morning. It was a different tune last night," Celia said.

"Oh you wouldn't need to mind me on a Friday night, the place gets so crowded and they're coming at you from all sides. I probably sounded a bit impatient, but didn't I thank you for doing the glasses, didn't I bring you a cup of tea in bed?" She was pleading now, almost like a child.

Celia took the bucket and the brush away from her gently and closed the door behind her. She lulled her to the table with soft talk. She didn't want the woman to bolt from the room.

"Of course you brought me a cup of tea in bed, and I *know* that deep down somewhere you are grateful to me for coming back and helping out, but that's not the point, Mam, not the point at all. You don't remember anything about last night, not from about nine o'clock on, that's what I'd say."

"What are you talking about?"

"You were well gone when I arrived – that was before ten. You fought with a man and said he'd only given you a fiver not a ten. You told young Biddy Brady that you didn't want a whole crowd of her girl friends cluttering up the pub tomorrow – fortunately Bart got us out of that one. You spilled a whole bottle of lime juice and you wouldn't let anyone wipe it up so that the counter was sticky all night. You couldn't find the tin of potato crisps and you told a group who had come here for the golfing that you didn't give a damn whether you found them or not, because they smelled to you like a child's fart. Yes, Mam, that's what you said."

Her mother looked up at her across the table. She showed no signs of getting up to run away. She looked at Celia quite calmly.

"I don't know why you are saying all this," she said.

"Because it happened, Mam." Celia begged her. "Believe me, it all happened, and more and much more other nights."

"And why would you make this up?"

"I didn't. It was like that; it will be like that again tonight, Mam, you're not able to cope. You've had a drink already today, I can see. I'm only telling you for your own good."

"Don't be ridiculous, Celia." She was about to stand up. Celia reached out and held her there. Hard by the wrist.

"I haven't written to the others yet: I didn't want to alarm them, I thought it might pass. I thought it was only weekends when you were under a bit of pressure. Mam, you have to accept it and DO something about it."

"Others?"

"Maura, Harry, Dan."

You're going to write all over the world with these tales?"

"Not if you can help yourself first. Mam, you're drinking far too much, you can't control it. What you're going to have to do is . . . "

"'I'm going to have to do nothing, thank you very much indeed. I may have had one too many sometimes and all right I'll watch that. Now will that satisfy you? Is the interrogation over? Can we get on with the day?"

"PLEASE Mam, listen. Anyone will tell you, will I get Bart in here to tell you what it's been like? Mrs Casey was saying, Billy Burns was saying, they were all saying . . . it's getting too much for you here . . . "

"You were always prudish about drink, Celia, even when your father was alive. You didn't realise that in a bar you have to be sociable and drink with the customers and be pleasant. You're not cut out for a pub the way we were, the way I am. You're too solemn, too sticky for people. That's always been your mistake."

There was no point in putting *Closed* on the door, she

wouldn't talk. The most she would admit was a drop too much on some occasions. She denied all the scenes, she remembered none of the conversations.

People started drifting in around lunchtime. Celia watched her mother accept a small whiskey from Dr Burke who had come in to get some drink to celebrate his son's engagement. Celia wished that Dee's father would lean over the counter to her mother and say "Mrs Ryan, your eyes are all bloodshot and there are big lines under them; for your health's sake you must give up drink." She wished that Father O'Reilly would come down from the presbytery on a home visit and tell her that for the good of her soul she must go and have some treatment and then take the pledge. But doctors and priests didn't interfere enough these days maybe.

The phone box was way at the end of the bar, quiet and discreet. No wonder half of Rathdoon made their calls from there rather than beside the eager ears of the post office people.

Emer was just getting the lunch. They had all been to the pictures last night on her winnings and tonight they might go again. Videos had gone through the roof: even the kids realised that a video was out of the question.

"What will I do with her?" Celia asked.

"She doesn't admit it to herself?"

"No. I gave her chapter and verse – what she said, what she spilled and broke, who she insulted. Not a word does she believe."

"And you can't get support troops in."

"Not really. Bart will be too polite and anyone else would be embarrassed."

"I suppose you'll have to wait."

"I can't wait any more and neither can she. It's terrible. There MUST be some way. How do people come to see things? Is there no way of hurrying it up?"

"Well, I did hear of a man who signed himself in for treatment the moment he saw himself on a video of his

175

daughter's wedding. He had no idea that he was so bad until . . . "

"That's it. Thanks Emer."

"WHAT? You're going to turn a video on your mother in Rathdoon? Have sense."

"I'll tell you about it on Monday." Celia was gone.

Mrs Fitzgerald invited her in. Yes, Tom was here. They were having a pot of coffee – would Celia join them? She felt they had been having a chat, that she shouldn't interrupt. She said she'd only be a minute. Yes he did have a small cassette recorder, and yes a blank tape . . . or a tape that she could record over. What was it – something from the radio? No, OK, it didn't matter. Look, it was easy to work. No, he didn't mind being without it until they were on the bus again. He was puzzled, but he didn't ask any more. She took it back to the pub.

There was so much clutter under the pub counter that the small tape recorder passed unnoticed.

Celia used it judiciously, half an hour on one side and half an hour on the other.

She even moved it out in her hand to be closer to her mother when the solo singing began and Mrs Ryan was screaming a tuneless racy version of a song which she hardly knew. She let it play for the insults to Bart Kennedy and for the bad language.

At one stage Tom Fitzgerald came into the bar, he saw his recorder and said "Is that fair?"

"You have your standards, I'll have mine," she snapped, and then much more wearily: "She doesn't know, you see, she really doesn't know."

"She's not going to like it," he said.

"No."

"When will you . . . ?"

"Tomorrow morning, I'd say."

"I'll come in around lunch and pick up the pieces," he smiled. He had a very, very nice smile.

Her mother sat stonily through the first few minutes. She railed with anger at the arguments and the bad language. Then she decided it was a fake and when she heard her maudlin conversation about what a great man her husband had been, tears of shame came into her eyes.

She folded her hands on her lap and sat like some timid employee waiting to be fired.

Out of the little tape recorder came the voice of Mrs Ryan as it called on Biddy Brady's engagement party to shut up and let HER sing. Tears fell from her closed eyes as the voice came out in its drunken, tuneless wail. Celia started to turn it off.

"Leave it," her mother said.

There was a long silence.

"Yes," said Mrs Ryan, "I see."

"If you wanted to, we could say you had pneumonia or that you were off to see Dan in Cowley. That would sort of cover it up."

"There'd be no point in covering it up. I mean, it's only more lies isn't it? Might as well say what it is." Her face was bleak.

"Sure you're half way there, Mam, if that's the way you think – you're nearly better," said Celia, leaning across the small dark tape recorder to hold her mother's hand.

Tom

He remembered the day he painted the Lilac Bus. It had been a sort of dirty beige before, and there was an exhilaration about pointing the spray can at it and seeing it change before his eyes. His mother had been appalled. It looked so vulgar and called attention to itself. That was about the worst crime in her book – attracting attention. The good went by unnoticed and understated; the bad were flashy and loud and painted their vans this silly mauve colour. Tom's father just shrugged. What could you expect? he asked his wife in a tone that meant the one thing he really didn't expect was an answer. Tom's father hardly ever spoke *to* Tom anymore: he spoke about him, in his hearing.

"I suppose that boy believes that money grows on trees . . . that boy thinks we should have the itinerants living in our garden . . . that boy feels that work is beneath him." Sometimes Tom answered; sometimes he let it pass. It didn't really matter which he did. His father's mind was fixed anyway: that boy was a waster, a left-wing long-haired layabout. A purple minibus was only what you'd expect.

It wasn't what Tom expected. He just decided one day on a whim, one day when the washing didn't seem to be making the van look any better. And he LOVED it now that it was lilac-coloured: it had much more personality and more life. That was when he decided to go into the transport business. It wasn't *exactly* legal of course, but suppose they did have an accident: an insurance company would have a hard time proving that he wasn't driving seven friends home for the weekend. No money was ever seen to change hands in Dublin. He didn't stand at the door selling tickets as the bigger bus people did. They were the same people all the time, give or take one or two a month. It wasn't a moneyspinner or anything; he paid for his petrol and cigarettes out of it, that was all. But it did mean he could smoke as much as he liked and he could come home every weekend to Rathdoon, which was what he wanted to do. The Lilac Bus had made all this possible.

Tom knew all about his passengers' lives in Rathdoon, but very little about what they did in Dublin. He had thought of finding out where they all lived and dropping them home rather than leaving them in the city centre at ten o'clock on a Sunday night but something told him that they might prefer the anonymity of the city to be kept absolute; they mightn't want the others to see their digs or their rooming houses or their set-up. More than once Tom had noticed a small fair-haired fellow in tinted glasses in a car parked near where the bus began and ended its weekend run. He would wave eagerly to Rupert Green. Now Rupert very clearly might not want that known. It was only because Tom had X-ray eyes that he had noticed the car. And his eyes had sometimes caught Dee Burke slipping into a big car and the arms of an older man. The older man had never been mentioned by Dee or by anyone in Rathdoon, so it was safe to assume that he was a secret older man not a legit one. No amount of watching or guessing could tell him what young Kev Kennedy was so afraid of. It hadn't always been that way: he used to be a very nice young fellow, and the only one of that family to get up from the kitchen table and leave their father and their slices of bread and ham and the radio on from Goodmorning to Closedown. But for the past year or so he was in bits.

Celia lived in a nurses' house. Six of them shared a place which was apparently highly successful. They had two television sets, a washing machine and an ironing board always in position in the back room. Celia had said there was never a cross word exchanged in that house – it was an ideal way to live until they married and had homes of their own. Nancy Morris shared a flat with that nice bouncy Mairead Hely; how Mairead stuck it was a mystery. He had met her one night at a party and she told him that Nancy's newest trick was to watch out for food tastings in supermarkets and rush in before they closed and have paper cups of soup or bits of cheese on toothpicks and then to come home triumphantly to the flat and say "I've had my supper." That night, and it was about three months back, Mairead had said that she was gathering up her courage to ask Nancy to leave, but she couldn't have gathered it yet. Poor Mikey was so nice Tom would have driven him home willingly, but he just laughed and walked to a bus stop with the never failing sense of good humour that was so hard to take. Judy Hickey took a bus the same direction and Tom often saw them talking together as he turned the Lilac Bus and drove off home.

None of them knew where his home was, that was certain. Long ago he had developed a gift for not answering direct questions so skilfully that people thought they had been given some kind of answer but didn't ask again. When Nancy Morris had asked him how much he paid a week for his flat, he said it was hard to work out, and that was that from Miss Morris. Rupert once asked him which side of the city did he live, and Tom had said that he was sure Rupert must know the trends in what people wanted. He often thought that it was interesting looking at people in cinema queues for example and wondering where they lived; he suposed that if he were working in an auctioneer's like Rupert, he'd think it even more interesting. Rupert agreed and had talked cheerfully about the unexpected ambitions of a lot of the people who came into his office. He never again asked Tom where he lived, and he didn't sound as if he had been rebuffed.

Dee Burke had told him that her brother was living in sin and wasn't it monstrous that boys could get away with it and girls still couldn't really. She had asked him suddenly, "Maybe you live in sin too. Do you?" "I don't know," he had said, "I'm very confused about sin; they never explained it properly at our school, what about yours?" Dee had said gloomily that they never stopped explaining it at her school and they were all so sick of it by the time they left, they had hardly the energy to commit any, which might have been the aim all along. But she still didn't find out what his lifestyle was. And down in Rathdoon he was spoken of as the one Fitzgerald boy that didn't join the family firm, the only one who didn't want to build an empire. He did something arty up in Dublin. But in any gathering of three if his name came up there would be three different theories on what he did. It gave the lie to the obsession with gossip that small towns were meant to have automatically, Tom thought. There was Dee with her older chap, Rupert with his boy friend, Kev with his gambling debts or whatever it was and no one back home knew a thing about any of them. Or about Tom. In Rathdoon only one person knew how Tom lived and why: his mother.

Nobody would guess that in a million years. His mother tutted with the best, sighed over his clothes and bus – genuine sighs. She really would have preferred a nice inconspicuous bus and more conservative clothes: nice neutral colours, stone-coloured trousers and brown jackets like her other sons wore. Suits, white shirts, restrained ties for Mass on Sunday. When his father railed about the young generation in general and That Boy in particular Tom's mother was gentle in her reproach. Anyone looking on might have thought she agreed with her husband. Who could have known that Tom was her lifeline?

She was a handsome woman, Peg Fitzgerald. Fifty-two, very well groomed; you never saw a hair out of place on Mrs Fitzgerald. She wore knitted suits, in lilacs or dark green, and a good brooch to tone in with whatever colour it was. In summer she wore lighter linen suits but they were the same colours and she had looked the same for years. She had three perms a year in the big town, and she had a shampoo and set every Friday morning of her life with little Sheila O'Reilly, the niece of the Parish Priest. Sheila didn't do much business in Rathdoon, but she never seemed to mind. She was always cheerful and if there were no heads of hair to deal with she did knitting instead and made a little out of that as a sideline. She wished there were more regular customers like Mrs Fitzgerald, who wanted their hair done the same way at the same time every week.

Mrs Fitzgerald was in the shop every day. The craft shop side of it had been her idea and was very successful. Any time a tour bus stopped there was a heavy electronic buzzing of tills in the Fitzgerald Craft Centre. There were shawls, lengths of tweed, pottery – a very wide range to suit all tastes. It was also the place where the whole of Rathdoon bought birthday presents for each other. Peg had difficulty persuading the family that it was a good idea, but now they looked at her with a new respect. She was a firm believer too that things should be kept in the family. When the boys married it was understood that their wives would work there. In fact one potential daughter-in-law broke off the engagement because she said all she would get from the marriage contract was to be an unpaid shop worker instead of the bank official that she was. Tom had thought that showed some spirit but the rest of the family including the jilted brother all combined in thinking they had a lucky escape if that was going to be her attitude.

From the outset Tom had said he wouldn't work in the shop; there had been no fight about it, only scorn. He had said reasonably he thought that it was better for his three brothers and two sisters if they *knew* from the word go that he would not be joining them. Then they could make their own plans without any question marks hanging over him. He decided this as long ago as his school days. But they had thought it was like being an engine driver and took no notice. What he would like to do was go to Dublin and live. Just live, not necessarily DO anything until he found something he'd like to do, and then maybe America or Paris or Greece. If you didn't have high living standards and want a comfortable house and a lot of possessions and rich food you could live very cheaply. They had thought it was a phase.

He had got a lot of honours in his Leaving, much more than the brothers who were well on their way to being merchant princes: expanding to other towns, opening new branches, developing their mother's much mocked idea of a craft shop in other centres all over the west. Tom was pronounced brighter than any of them by the masters who had taught all the Fitzgeralds, but he was adamant and very firm for an eighteen year old. He had all these bits of paper to prove he was educated, now could he get on with his own life? He thanked his father as warmly as he could for the grudging offer of university fees, but still it was no. All he wanted was to be left alone. He wouldn't go to the bad, he would come home regularly if they liked so that they could see him and satisfy themselves that he was still normal. He would hitch. He would sign on for the dole each week, and NO that would not be an almighty disgrace in Dublin. Who would see him or know him for God's sake, and NO it was not unfair, that's what people did nowadays: the rich paid taxes and there was at least bread and a roof for those who weren't rich. We didn't let them die in the streets today, stepping over them saying wasn't it a pity they didn't have the get up and go to find a good job and earn their living. NO, he did not intend to stay on national assistance for ever. And, YES, he was very grateful for the offer of a place in the family firm but we only had one life and that was not how he was going to spend his.

And wasn't it lucky that this is what he had decided to do? What on earth would have happened if he hadn't been around?

It had been very easy to live cheaply in Dublin. For a

while he lived with a young couple who gave him a bed and some food; they didn't have all that much themselves. He taught their children every evening, two nice bright little boys. He went over everything they had done at school and helped them with their homework. But he didn't really like it because he felt they should be out playing instead of doing more and yet more. They knew enough, he kept telling their worried young parents, they're fine: don't pack their heads with facts and more and more. The parents didn't understand. Surely the best thing was to get a good start, to be in there with a better chance than the others? But they were only ten and nine, it was YEARS before they would need to be in there fighting the others for places and points and positions. No, the pale mother and father hadn't got on in their lives because they had nobody to guide them; they weren't going to let the same thing happen to the children. He left them amicably. He worked as a gardener for an old lady and slept in her garden shed for a year without her knowing. She never knew in the end, and he had moved his camp bed and primus stove long before the funeral so nobody ever knew.

He worked in a night club as a sort of bouncer. He was slim and not the typical bouncer material but he had a look in his eye that was as important as muscle. His boss who was one of the sharpest men in Dublin was anxious to keep him on, promote him even, but it wasn't the life Tom wanted. He left again amicably and before he left he asked the sharp boss what was good about him. He'd like to know just for his own record. The Boss said he owed him no explanation if he was leaving but OK, Tom had a look in his eye that said he would go the distance. People didn't mess with him. Tom liked this reference just as he had liked the old lady saying he was a loving sort of gardener, and the nine year old boy saying that he made Latin so much more interesting than they did at school because there was none of this treating it as a language – more as a puzzle really. But these were not written references. Each new job had to be found on charm or effort; each time he had to go in cold.

He had a summer in Greeece driving a minibus, not unlike the lilac bus, over mountainy roads, taking holidaymakers to and from airport and hotels. He had a summer in America working at a children's camp with seventy discontented youngsters who would all rather have been at home. He had a winter in Amsterdam working in a souvenir shop. He had a funny three months in London working in market surveys – going up to people on the street with a clipboard and asking them questions. He had a different kind of three months in London working as a hospital orderly; he found it harrowing, and his respect for nurses went way, way up. He had been on the point of telling Celia about those months, several times, but he never told stories about what he had done – it led to questions and questions often needed answers.

He didn't think of himself as a drifter, and yet for nine years, since he had left school, he had done nothing with any purpose or any permanence. Still, he wouldn't have missed any of it, not even those strange days in the hospital pushing elderly frightened people on trolleys through crowds, all speaking different languages, all the nationalities under the sun working in the hospital and coming in as patients. And now it meant that he could look after Phil, for he had no job to give up, no real lifestyle to interrupt.

Phil was the nicest in his family, there was no doubt about it. They all agreed on that, just as they all agreed that Tom was the oddest and the most difficult. Phil was the nearest to him in age: she was almost a year to the day older than he was. All the six Fitzgeralds arrived within seven years, and then the young Peg stopped producing a new baby every season. There were pictures of them all when they were toddlers and Tom always thought it looked like a nursery school rather than one family. But his mother had always said it was great to get it all over at once. You had a period when they all seemed to be unmanageable and then suddenly they had all grown up. Anyway Phil had always been his special friend, and in the great sixteen and seventeen year old arguments about Tom not joining the firm Phil had been very supportive. She had been in the big town seventeen miles from Rathdoon learning shorthand and typing at the time, it had been agreed that she should work in the office rather than the shop. But she used to come home at weekends during her commercial course and encourage Tom to live his own life. She had a big round face, Phil had, and she was always laughing. Years ago he remembered her dancing with Red Kennedy and getting a lecture that the Kennedys were perfectly nice, not a thing wrong with them, but she should set her sights a little higher. Phil had said indignantly that she wasn't setting her sights at Red Kennedy or at anyone, she was just dancing with him, but there had still been a lot of head shaking.

Phil was what they called a fine girl in Rathdoon, Mrs Fitzgerald used to say that she'd slim down when the time came. Hadn't Anna, the eldest of the family had a lot of puppy fat too. But Mrs Fitzgerald always thought that there was some kind of law which said that a girl needed to be nice and slim and attractive when she was thinking of choosing a husband and settling down. It was just the way things were. But Phil didn't notice some magical trick of nature: she remained plump and round-faced and never developed the hollow cheeks and small waist which were generally agreed to have been important when her sister Anna attracted and married the very suitable Dominic whose family made tweeds.

Tom had never thought she was too fat; he had told her that several times when he came home for the weekend. He said she must be losing her marbles to think she was a fatty, and cracked to think that she had no friends because of this.

"Who are my friends then? List them," she had cried.

Tom couldn't, but he said he couldn't list any friends of his family for God's sake, he was away, he didn't live here. She MUST have friends. No, she claimed, she didn't. That was when meaning to be helpful he had suggested this

Singles type of holiday. Everyone went on their own, there were no loving couples to start out with but hopefully plenty of them on the way back. Phil had read the brochure eagerly and decided that she should go on it.

"Don't tell anyone it's a singles special," her mother had advised. "It looks a little pathetic. Say it's an ordinary holiday in Spain."

Tom never knew quite what happened, but it wasn't a success. Phil said that Spain was all right, and the weather had been fair, but nothing else. Later, much later, he heard that all the girls except Phil had been topless on the beaches, that almost everyone on the group charter had enjoyed a close physical relationship with one or more other people on the same group charter – again, everyone except Phil – and that there was no question of meeting people and dancing with them and talking to them and getting to know them. This was apparently a much more swinging type of holiday than some singles outings, and swinging meant going to bed with people, people who were total strangers.

But Tom didn't know all this at the time. Phil had come back quiet and non-communicative. He noticed shortly after this that she seemed to have lost weight, but he didn't say anything, because he had been the one to tell her that weight wasn't important. If he admired her now, she would believe that he had only been kind before. Phil didn't go to the dance any more and she didn't go out to the sea with a crowd of girls like she used to. But to be honest, he didn't notice these things at the time; it was only afterwards he remembered it all.

Phil had come to Dublin on one of the day excursions by train from the town. It was a bit of a killer: the train left at 9 a.m., you were in Dublin at noon and then the train back was at 6 p.m. So it was some concentrated shopping before they all fell back with sore feet and bulging parcels to go home again that night. Phil always rang Tom if she went on one of these marathons, and he came to meet her at the station in his minibus which was a dirty beige in those days.

She looked very pale, and said that she had been having really terrible pains like a knife on the train, so bad that the people in her carriage said she should go to a hospital or a doctor since she had been crying out with the sharpness of them. Tom looked concerned and just at that moment she bent over again doubled up with pain and letting out a long low scream, so his mind was made up. He drove her to the out-patients of a hospital. He was quiet and firm. He got her seen before anyone by saying it was an emergency. As her brother, he signed the permission to operate for a burst appendix and he was there when she woke up to tell her that it had all been fine, and it was over and all she had to do now was to rest. Her troubled face smiled at him sadly. Their mother came up the next day with a suitcase of things that Phil would need, a lot of reassurance, sighs of how good God was to let it all happen when Tom was there to take charge, and messages of love, boxes of chocolates, bottles of lavender water from the rest of the family.

She was recovering quite well Tom thought. Well, her strength was coming back quickly and he was very startled when one of the nurses said she would like to talk to him about his sister. Privately. She had made a report to the people who should know already, like the matron and the surgeon who had operated, but this was now something that must be taken further, through Miss Fitgerald's own doctor perhaps.

He was alarmed. The nurse spoke reprovingly, as if poor Phil had been caught stealing in the wards. What was it? Well, the nurse had noticed she spent a long time at the lavatory, and she had asked her about constipation or diarrhoea. Apparently neither, but she was still in there for a considerable time, so the nurse had listened at the door. Tom felt his heart beating: what horror was he going to be told?

It was what the nurse had suspected. Vomiting, retching. Two or three times a day.

"What's causing it?" Tom cried. He had no idea what

the tone of shock was all about. Why wasn't he being told this by a doctor?

"She's doing it herself," the nurse said. "Eating chocolates, biscuits, banana, slices of bread and butter. You should have seen the papers and the empty boxes. And then vomiting it all up."

"But why on earth would she do that?"

"It's called Bulimia; it's like anorexia nervosa – you know, where people starve themselves to death if they can. It's a form of it. They binge and gorge and then they make themselves sick to get rid of the food they've eaten."

"Phil does this?"

"Yes, she's been doing it for some time."

"And did this cause her appendix to burst?"

"Oh no, not at all, that was something totally unconnected. But maybe lucky in a way. Because at least now you know and the family will know and help her try to fight it."

"Can't you just tell her to stop. Can't we all tell her it's . . . it's revolting – it's so senseless."

'Oh no, that's not the way, that's not what they'll say at all when she goes in."

"Goes in where?"

"To a pyschiatric hospital. It's a mental condition, you know, it's got nothing to do with us."

The nurse wasn't quite correct. It did have a little to do with them because Phil was admitted to the psychiatric wing of that same hospital and there was a medical side to her treatment as well as all the therapy and group discussions on the psychiatric side. She had been very relieved at the beginning to know that other people did the same thing. She thought she was the only person in the world who had ever done it, and she felt a great burden of guilt taken off her shoulders. She never felt guilty about the self-induced vomiting: she said it was the easiest thing in the world. If you just put your finger in the right place down your throat it happened automatically. But she did feel guilty about stuffing herself with the food. Especially eating in a lavatory – that was the thing she felt shameful about. She wasn't ready at all to talk about why she did it. Tom was told that she would undoubtedly do it again and again before she was cured. Before she came back to reality and accepted that she was perfectly fine as she was. The help and support of a family at a time like this was crucial. If Phil was to see that she was a person of high esteem in her own family that would go a very long way towards helping her have a good image of herself again. The family, yes. But Lord God the Fitzgerald family. At this time.

Poor Phil couldn't have picked a worse time to call on them, Tom thought grimly. It was the very period that the newspapers were full of the case about the armed raid on the post office in Cork and the subsequent conviction and sentencing of Teddy Fitzgerald their cousin, who had worked in the business with the family. That had been a heavy cross. Then there was the infidelity of Dominic, the highly suitable husband of Anna the eldest. There had been many a tale of a relationship and finally the birth of a child which Dominic grudgingly acknowledged as his, even though it was born not to his wife but to one of the most unsuitable women in the west of Ireland, tinkers who had settled down and according to Mrs Peg Fitzgerald the only thing worse than a tinker on the road was a tinker who had settled down. So there was that disgrace. And there had been a few other things too, none of them as shocking but all of them adding up to a general family anxiety. It was the wrong time to hear that a member of the family was now entering on to a long period of psychiatric treatment and would need their support.

Mrs Fitzgerald made her point of view absolutely clear. There would be no talk about Phil whatsoever. This was final. Phil had recovered from her burst appendix, she had been convalescing, she had been visiting friends, she would come back shortly. Meanwhile they would get a temporary girl for the office. Mrs Fitzgerald would go to Dublin once a month to give this support that the hospital said it needed, Tom would go to see her as often as he could, and that was it. It would not be discussed; they had quite enough problems already without adding this one. And what would it do to Phil's chances of getting a husband if it was widely known she had been in a mental institution? No more arguments.

Tom was sure that this was not what the doctors meant by family support: hushing it all up, making it into a greater shame than Phil already felt it was. He was certain that his mother's monthly visits – full of assurances that nobody knew, no one suspected, people had been fooled and hoodwinked, cover stories had been invented – were all the worst thing for his sister who would listen with stricken face and apologise for all the trouble she had caused. Sometimes his mother would reach out awkwardly and take Phil's hand.

"We love you ... um ... very much. You are much loved, Phil." Then she would draw her hand back, embarrassed. She had been told by the psychiatrist that this was a good line to emphasise, but she recited it as if it were learned by heart. They were not a demonstrative family, they had never hugged or kissed each other. It was hard for his mother to reach out and say that to Phil. And bewildering for Phil to hear it, just before her mother gathered her gloves and handbag and started to leave.

He went to see Phil every day, every single day and he telephoned her on each Saturday and Sunday. His mother said that she would telephone except that there was nothing to say, but Tom found things. After all he knew her much better: they had been meeting each other constantly, and he was able to pick from a variety of things to say. He never felt as if he were talking to someone who wasn't well. He didn't talk down to her, he would never apologise profusely if he hadn't been able to ring or visit, just briefly. He wouldn't let on that he thought his presence was essential to her. He treated her as if she were as sane as he was.

They talked about childhood a lot. Tom remembered his as happy enough, too much talk about the business, a bit too much of covering over and not letting the neighbours know this or that, and keeping our business to ourselves. Phil remembered it quite differently. She remembered that they were always laughing, and that they had all been sitting round the table together talking to each other, though Tom said they couldn't have been. There would have to have been either their mother or their father in the shop. Phil remembered them going on great outings to the sea and picnics; Tom said he honestly could only remember one. Phil said they used to play games like I Spy and the Minister's Cat, and Sardines, where one person had to hide and when you found them you squeezed in like a sardine beside them. Tom said that was only at parties. But they didn't fight over the memories; they talked them over like an old film that you'd seen years ago and everyone could remember bits of, but nobody could remember all of.

They talked about boyfriends and girlfriends and sex. Tom wasn't surprised to hear that she was a virgin, and she wasn't surprised to hear that he was not. They talked easily and without guilt, sometimes for hours in the day room or in the garden, sometimes just for short times because Phil was silent and withdrawn, or because Tom had to work. He was working in an auction showroom these days, helping to carry furniture in and out, put lot numbers on things and write them up in a catalogue. He had been thinking of moving on, but the hours suited him and it was near the hospital so that he could come and go easily. One of the other patients asked if Tom was her boyfriend. She had laughed uneasily and said she never had a boyfriend. The other girl had shrugged and said she was probably as well off: they were a barrel full of trouble that's all they were. She hadn't assumed for a moment that Phil COULDN'T have a boyfriend. It made Phil feel a lot more cheerful. She asked Tom what kind of girls he liked, and he said unusual ones, not people who talked about houses and engagement rings and the Future. He had a very nice girlfriend once but unfortunately she met a really dull guy and he offered her all this other business – security, respectability – and she came and told Tom straight out she was going to take it. Phil had been very sympathetic.

"You never told us any of this," she said.

"True, but you never told us that you half fancied Billy Burns, even though he was a married man," he said laughing.

"You dragged that out of me" she laughed too. He thought it was all too slow, she MUST be better now.

He said this more than once to the psychiatrist and was depressed to hear that Phil was still not happy, still not at ease with herself and sure of her place in the world. They all thanked Tom for coming and said he was invaluable. Not only in his own visits but in the lifeline he offered back to Rathdoon. She never minded his going back home at weekends. In fact she liked it because it brought her closer to the family and because he always brought back news of them all and, better still, a cheerful letter from her mother.

Every Saturday morning he forced his mother to write her a letter. He literally sat there while she wrote. He wouldn't accept that she had nothing to write about, and he refused to let her wriggle out of it.

"Do you think I'd be doing this, do you think I'd sit here every Saturday morning unless it was important?" he had shouted. "She is desperate to know that we are fond of her, and that her place is here; she won't be ABLE to come back unless she knows this."

"But of course it's here, naturally we want her back. For heaven's sake, Tom, you're making a big drama out of it all."

"It is a big drama. Phil is in a psychiatric hospital and mainly because we can't let her know that she is important here."

"Your father and I think that's all mumbo jumbo. She was never made to feel anything but important; we treated her with great respect, people loved having her in the office. She was always so cheerful, and she knew everyone's names: wasn't she the life and soul of that place?"

"Write it. Write it down on paper," he would order.

"I'd feel stupid saying that to Phil. It's silly, it's treating her as if she's not all there. She'll know I'm only acting."

"But you said you meant it, a minute ago."

'Yes, of course I mean it, but it's not something you say, not something you write down."

"Since you're not there to say it, you have to write it. Since you won't let her come home and be treated in the town where you'd only be seventeen miles away, where you could see her every day, then you're going to have to write it. Otherwise how is she to know, how in God's earth can she KNOW that she's important here?"

"It's not that I won't let her come back here. It's for her own good, to keep things quiet, to keep our business to ourselves." He had heard it so often, maybe he would hear it for ever. Perhaps Phil would never get better.

He was in the middle of yet another Saturday confrontation when Celia Ryan came in. He was surprised to see her, and in a way relieved. His mother had been very hard to pin down today. She had escaped him in the morning by saying she was needed in the shop, and it was only when he brought her a cup of coffee and a writing pad that he could get her to listen. She had been going through one of her Phil-must-pull-herself-together phases. Tom felt a mad urge to ask Celia to sit down and explain to his mother her own first-hand knowledge of Anorexia and Bulimia, mentioning casually that Phil was in a psychiatric ward with the latter. His mother would probably fall senseless to the ground if he were to tell the family disgrace to Mrs Ryan's daughter. The temptation had only been a flicker.

Celia wanted a loan of his tape recorder, of all things,

and a blank cassette. She wanted to record something. She seemed flustered. She didn't tell him what she wanted it for, but then he rarely told people anything, whether they asked him or not, so he couldn't fault her there. She said she'd give it to him on the bus.

"Terrible time she has with that mother of hers," Mrs Fitzgerald said.

Tom nodded. He thought he didn't have a great time with his own mother but it was not in him to say it; he just wanted the letter to give to Phil on Monday.

"She'll probably marry Bart Kennedy, and they can keep an eye on the place that way," Tom said.

"Bart Kennedy? Not at all. Sure nobody will marry Bart Kennedy, he's not the type that marries." Mrs Fitzgerald was positive.

"Bart, a fairy? Go on out of that."

"No, I don't mean that or anything like it. He's just not the kind of man who marries, you must see that. Maybe men don't notice these things: women do. Red Kennedy now, he'll be married within the year I'd say, I hear he's courting. But Bart – not at all."

"I thought that's what she came home for," Tom said.

"She comes home to stop that place going down the drain, that's all."

"Really?" Tom felt pleased. He didn't know why but he felt a sense of relief.

He went into the pub that night and discovered why she had wanted the tape recorder. It seemed a bit sneaky somehow. Like taking advantage of the poor woman who was slobbering and messing around behind her own bar. Even more humiliating was the thought that Mrs Ryan's daughter was recording the tuneless singing.

"She doesn't know, she really doesn't know," Celia said as an explanation when he had asked her was it fair. He imagined Celia trying to tell her mother about the excesses of the night before and Mrs Ryan brushing it away with that busines-like cheerful manner she had when sober. It wasn't the kind of thing anyone else would say to her so she would be bound to believe that Celia was making it up at worst or at the very least exaggerating it.

"I'll come round tomorrow and pick up the pieces," he said. She smiled back at him, a warm grateful smile. He looked at Bart Kennedy. Bart was pulling pints and laughing with the lads – he and Celia didn't have eyes for each other at all. Tom must have been mad to have thought it in the first place.

There were no pieces to pick up next day. Celia's mother had taken it very well. She was sitting in the back room while Celia and Bart dealt with the Sunday lunchtime trade.

"She's coming to Dublin. I thought it would be easier. I'd be able to get to see her."

"When?"

"Tomorrow. I won't come back on the bus tonight. I'll wait and go with her. I've a great friend, a nurse in Dublin – she'll work for me tomorrow even though it's meant to be her day off."

"Does she live in your harem of nurses?"

"Emer? Not at all: she's a respectable married woman with a family."

"Would you work if you were married?"

"Bloody sure I would. Catch me giving up a job to cook meals and clean a house for a man. Anyway everyone has to nowadays. How would you have any life at all if you didn't? And nursing's fine, I'd hate to lose it."

"How long will it be . . ." he nodded towards the back room where Mrs Ryan sat waiting in a chair.

"I don't know. It depends on her – you know, if she wants to."

"Doesn't it depend on her family too, and support?"

"Well there's only me; she can't have the beauties in Australia and Detroit and England, so she'll have to make do with me."

"My sister Phil isn't well, she's got the same problem,"

he said suddenly.

"I never knew Phil had a drink problem." She said it without censure or shock.

"No, not that, I meant she has the same problem: she only has me in Dublin. She's got an anorexic thing, you know, but she does eat and makes herself vomit."

"She's a better chance with that; so many of the anorexics die, it's desperate to see them, little wizened monkeys, and they think that this is the best way to be. But bulimia is very stressful, poor Phil. Isn't that very bad luck."

He looked at her gratefully. "Will they be any help, the ones who've gone away?"

"I shouldn't think so, will yours?"

"No. I'm beginning to realise it now. I kept thinking I could change them, but it's all head in the sand, pretend it isn't happening, don't tell anyone."

"In time, in their time maybe. Not yours." She was very gentle.

"Well they'll have to make do with us then," he said, "your half mad Ma and my half mad sister."

"Aren't they lucky they've got us," said Celia Ryan and laughed like a peal of bells.

"I'll miss you going back on the bus tonight," he said.

"Well maybe you might come and console me when I've got my mother in. And if it would be any help I could come and see Phil with you, if you'd like it, that is?"

"I'd like it a lot," said Tom Fitzgerald.

Bestselling Women's Fiction

☐ Destinies	Charlotte Vale Allen	£2.95
☐ Hester Dark	Emma Blair	£1.95
☐ Nellie Wildchild	Emma Blair	£2.50
☐ Playing the Jack	Mary Brown	£3.50
☐ Twin of Fire	Jude Deveraux	£2.50
☐ Counterfeit Lady	Jude Deveraux	£2.50
☐ Miss Gathercole's Girls	Judy Gardiner	£2.50
☐ Lisa Logan	Marie Joseph	£1.95
☐ Maggie Craig	Marie Joseph	£1.95
☐ A Long Way From Heaven	Sheelagh Kelly	£2.95
☐ The Gooding Girl	Pamela Oldfield	£2.75
☐ The Running Years	Claire Rayner	£2.75
☐ The Pride	Judith Saxton	£2.50

NAME ....

ADDRESS ....

....

....

U.K. CUSTOMERS: Please allow 22p per book to a maximum of £3.00.

B.F.P.O. & EIRE: Please allow 22p per book to a maximum of £3.00.

OVERSEAS CUSTOMERS: Please allow 22p per book.

Whilst every effort is made to keep prices low it is sometimes necessary to increase cover prices at short notice. Arrow Books reserve the right to show new retail prices on covers which may differ from those previously advertised in the text or elsewhere.

Bestselling Fiction

☐ Dancing Bear	Chaim Bermant	£2.95
☐ Hiroshima Joe	Martin Booth	£2.95
☐ 1985	Anthony Burgess	£1.95
☐ The Other Woman	Colette	£1.95
☐ The Manchurian Candidate	Richard Condon	£2.25
☐ Letter to a Child Never Born	Oriana Fallaci	£1.25
☐ Duncton Wood	William Horwood	£3.50
☐ Aztec	Gary Jennings	£3.95
☐ The Journeyer	Gary Jennings	£3.50
☐ The Executioner's Song	Norman Mailer	£3.50
☐ Strumpet City	James Plunkett	£3.50
☐ Admiral	Dudley Pope	£1.95
☐ The Second Lady	Irving Wallace	£2.50
☐ An Unkindness of Ravens	Ruth Rendell	£1.95
☐ The History Man	Malcolm Bradbury	£2.95

NAME ....

ADDRESS ....

....

....

U.K. CUSTOMERS: Please allow 22p per book to a maximum of £3.00.

B.F.P.O. & EIRE: Please allow 22p per book to a maximum of £3.00.

OVERSEAS CUSTOMERS: Please allow 22p per book.

Whilst every effort is made to keep prices low it is sometimes necessary to increase cover prices at short notice. Arrow Books reserve the right to show new retail prices on covers which may differ from those previously advertised in the text or elsewhere.

Bestselling Thriller/Suspense

☐ Voices on the Wind	Evelyn Anthony	£2.50
☐ See You Later, Alligator	William F. Buckley	£2.50
☐ Hell is Always Today	Jack Higgins	£1.75
☐ Brought in Dead	Harry Patterson	£1.95
☐ The Graveyard Shift	Harry Patterson	£1.95
☐ Maxwell's Train	Christopher Hyde	£2.50
☐ Russian Spring	Dennis Jones	£2.50
☐ Nightbloom	Herbert Lieberman	£2.50
☐ Basikasingo	John Matthews	£2.95
☐ The Secret Lovers	Charles McCarry	£2.50
☐ Fletch	Gregory McDonald	£1.95
☐ Green Monday	Michael M. Thomas	£2.95
☐ Someone Else's Money	Michael M. Thomas	£2.50
☐ Albatross	Evelyn Anthony	£2.50
☐ The Avenue of the Dead	Evelyn Anthony	£2.50

NAME ....

ADDRESS ....

....

....

U.K. CUSTOMERS: Please allow 22p per book to a maximum of £3.00.

B.F.P.O. & EIRE: Please allow 22p per book to a maximum of £3.00.

OVERSEAS CUSTOMERS: Please allow 22p per book.

Whilst every effort is made to keep prices low it is sometimes necessary to increase cover prices at short notice. Arrow Books reserve the right to show new retail prices on covers which may differ from those previously advertised in the text or elsewhere.

Bestselling Humour

☐ Picking on Men Again	Judy Allen & Dyan Sheldon	£1.95
☐ Carrott Roots	Jasper Carrott	£3.50
☐ A Little Zit on the Side	Jasper Carrott	£1.75
☐ The Corporate Infighter's Handbook	William Davis	£2.50
☐ The Art of Coarse Drinking	Michael Green	£1.95
☐ Armchair Anarchist's Handbook	Mike Harding	£2.95
☐ You Can See the Angel's Bum, Miss Worswick!	Mike Harding	£1.95
☐ Sex Tips for Girls	Cynthia Heimel	£2.50
☐ Lower than Vermin	Kevin Killane	£4.95
☐ More Tales from the Mess	Miles Noonan	£1.95
☐ Limericks	Michael Palin	£1.50
☐ Bodge It Yourself: The Beginner's Guide to BIY	Jeff Slapdash	£2.95
☐ Dieter's Guide to Weight Loss During Sex	Richard Smith	£1.95
☐ Tales From a Long Room	Peter Tinniswood	£1.95

NAME ....

ADDRESS ....

....

....

U.K. CUSTOMERS: Please allow 22p per book to a maximum of £3.00.

B.F.P.O. & EIRE: Please allow 22p per book to a maximum of £3.00.

OVERSEAS CUSTOMERS: Please allow 22p per book.

Bestselling Non-Fiction

☐ The Alexander Principle	Wilfred Barlow	£2.95
☐ The Complete Book of Exercises	Diagram Group	£4.95
☐ Everything is Negotiable	Gavin Kennedy	£2.95
☐ Health on Your Plate	Janet Pleshette	£2.50
☐ The Cheiro Book of Fate and Fortune	Cheiro	£2.95
☐ The Handbook of Chinese Horoscopes	Theodora Lau	£2.50
☐ Hollywood Babylon	Kenneth Anger	£7.95
☐ Hollywood Babylon II	Kenneth Anger	£7.95
☐ The Domesday Heritage	Ed. Elizabeth Hallam	£3.95
☐ Historic Railway Disasters	O. S. Nock	£2.50
☐ Wildlife of the Domestic Cat	Roger Tabor	£4.50
☐ Elvis and Me	Priscilla Presley	£2.95
☐ Maria Callas	Arianna Stassinopoulos	£2.50
☐ The Brendan Voyage	Tim Severin	£3.50

NAME ....

ADDRESS ....

....

....

U.K. CUSTOMERS: Please allow 22p per book to a maximum of £3.00.

B.F.P.O. & EIRE: Please allow 22p per book to a maximum of £3.00.

OVERSEAS CUSTOMERS: Please allow 22p per book.

Whilst every effort is made to keep prices low it is sometimes necessary to increase cover prices at short notice. Arrow Books reserve the right to show new retail prices on covers which may differ from those previously advertised in the text or elsewhere.

A Selection of Arrow Bestsellers

NAME ....

ADDRESS ....

....

....

U.K. CUSTOMERS: Please allow 22p per book to a maximum of £3.00.

B.F.P.O. & EIRE: Please allow 22p per book to a maximum of £3.00.

OVERSEAS CUSTOMERS: Please allow 22p per book.

Whilst every effort is made to keep prices low it is sometimes necessary to increase cover prices at short notice. Arrow Books reserve the right to show new retail prices on covers which may differ from those previously advertised in the text or elsewhere.

Arena

☐ The Lives of the Indian Princes	Charles Allen	£4.95
☐ Confessions of an Irish Rebel	Brendan Behan	£2.95
☐ Dancing Bear	Chaim Bermant	£2.95
☐ Let It Come Down	Paul Bowles	£2.95
☐ The After Dinner Game	Malcolm Bradbury	£1.95
☐ Eating People is Wrong	Malcolm Bradbury	£2.95
☐ Rates of Exchange	Malcolm Bradbury	£2.95
☐ So the Wind Won't Blow It All Away	Richard Brautigan	£2.95
☐ Ten Years in an Open Necked Shirt	John Cooper Clarke	£3.50
☐ The Wit and Wisdom of Quentin Crisp	Quentin Crisp	£2.50
☐ Thy Tears Might Cease	Michael Farrell	£2.95
☐ Boys on the Rock	John Fox	£2.50
☐ Selected Letters of E. M. Forster	Ed. Mary Lago & P. N. Furbank	£4.50
☐ Pudding and Pie (Nancy Mitford Omnibus)	Nancy Mitford	£3.95
☐ Mourners Below	James Purdy	£2.95

NAME . . . .

ADDRESS . . . .

. . . .

. . . .

U.K. CUSTOMERS: Please allow 22p per book to a maximum of £3.00.

B.F.P.O. & EIRE: Please allow 22p per book to a maximum of £3.00.

OVERSEAS CUSTOMERS: Please allow 22p per book.

Whilst every effort is made to keep prices low it is sometimes necessary to increase cover prices at short notice. Arrow Books reserve the right to show new retail prices on covers which may differ from those previously advertised in the text or elsewhere.

Arrow Health

NAME ....

ADDRESS ....

....

....

U.K. CUSTOMERS: Please allow 22p per book to a maximum of £3.00.

B.F.P.O. & EIRE: Please allow 22p per book to a maximum of £3.00.

OVERSEAS CUSTOMERS: Please allow 22p per book.

Whilst every effort is made to keep prices low it is sometimes necessary to increase cover prices at short notice. Arrow Books reserve the right to show new retail prices on covers which may differ from those previously advertised in the text or elsewhere.